The Collected Works *of* Noah Cicero

Volume 2

Lazy Fascist Press
Portland, OR

Lazy Fascist Press
an imprint of Eraserhead Press
PO Box 10065
Portland, OR 97296

www.lazyfascistpress.com

ISBN: 978-1-62105-148-0

Cover Design by Matthew Revert
www.matthewrevert.com

Printed in the USA.

Table of Contents

THE INSURGENT

BOOK 1

1.

I should kill myself.

Things would be better if I did.

For me anyway.

I don't know how it would affect global warming or penguins in Antarctica.

But it might help me.

I'm lying on the floor in my living room.

Curled up in the fetal position.

In the fetal position nothing can hurt me.

I'm safe.

Today is my day off.

I don't know what to do with myself.

Time will pass and another dreary day will come.

My sister Sasha is on the computer playing solitaire.

She looks dissatisfied.

She takes care of me.

No one else will.

Everyone wants me to die and go to hell and be burned for eternity.

I'm not even sure why.

This is so horrible.

Sasha says, "Vasily, what the fuck are you doing?"

"I'm hiding."

"From what?"

"That's none of your business."

"Have you heard?"

"Heard what, that God is dead and we are alone?"

"Somebody named Cho shot a bunch of people."

"Who the hell is Cho?"

"Cho is like the new superstar murderer."

"How many did he kill?"

"Thirty-two."

"That's not nearly enough to make a difference," I say.

"It says he made videos."

"Like on YouTube?"

"I don't know. Something like he made videos and rambled about how everyone hated him and shit."

"I don't need this."

Sasha gets up and goes into the kitchen. I don't know why she went in there. She seems to be doing something involving the refrigerator. I hear some liquid pouring.

I wonder if she is going to get a gun and kill me.

She should.

Killing me would be a good idea for her.

It would save her money.

I make only seven dollars an hour dishwashing at a steak-house.

She has to feed me most days.

I can't afford to live on this planet and eat.

I'm an atrocity to humankind.

Sasha returns from the kitchen and says, "Seriously, what is wrong? You've been on the floor for over an hour."

"I got a letter."

"What did it say?"

I pull the letter out of my pocket and hand it to her.

"Holy shit, Vasily, it says you owe the student loan people $10,000 and you have to pay it in one installment because you neglected to pay anything at all."

"Yes, I know what it fucking says."

"That's bad."

"My life is over. I am condemned to a life of misery. I will never succeed. Count me out of the game of life. I should kill myself."

"Don't say that. It reminds me of Lizaveta."

"Lizaveta is dead."

"I know Lizaveta is dead."

"She has chosen to be no more."

"You need to shut the fuck up," Sasha says.

Lizaveta is our sister. Or was our sister. Lizaveta killed herself. She has been dead for a good while. I miss her sometimes.

"Let's not talk about Lizaveta," Sasha says.

"That sounds good."

"So what are you going to do about this bill?"

"I suppose I'll wait it out."

"How are you going to wait it out?"

"I don't fucking know. Die."

"Die?"

"Yes, I'll fucking die and then I'll have no more $10,000 bill to pay back in one giant installment."

"That's not a good plan."

"You got a better one?"

"No, I can't think of anything."

"See, I'm fucked, I'm condemned, I'm ruined. My life on this planet is ruined."

"You're being dramatic."

"I can't be a doctor or a lawyer or president with a bill like that."

"No, that would be impossible."

"See, impossible. My life is caged in. There is no escape. I'm going to die poor, alone, and naked."

"And naked?"

"Yes, fucking naked!"

"Maybe you could get a better job."

"A better job? Doing what? I have no skills, I didn't finish college."

"That's true. You have no skills."

"I'll never get laid again."

2.

I'm sitting with Chang in his bathroom. Chang is in the bathtub washing himself. He is scrubbing like he is trying to remove his skin.

If you go to Chang's house, you will most likely have to talk to him while he is in the bathtub. Out of politeness, he takes a bubble bath so you don't have to see him fully naked. Even his parents have to endure this.

Chang looks at me and says, "You know why I'm washing myself, right?"

Chang does this routine about once a week.

"Yes, I know."

"You know, when I was little. When I was coming over on the boat from China, they stuck my family and me down in a dark black hole to live in. We weren't allowed out and there was no bathroom. So everyone shit in the corner of the room. It was horrible. The stink of shit was horrible. All you could smell was shit for weeks."

"That sounds horrible."

"Yes, it was terrible. But it became worse. My fucking brother Dong, that stupid asshole, decided to, out of a joke, throw me in the fucking shit!" Chang pauses for a second. A look of total anger comes over his face, then he goes, "My fucking brother threw me in the shit, then stood there laughing. Of course I was crying and screaming because I was five, and all he did was stand there laughing. Then my mother ran over in the darkness and beat the shit out of Dong, which almost made me feel better about being covered in shit, but didn't, and never has.

"My mother picked me up out of the shit and carried me back over to our little corner of the hole we were traveling in. We could not spare any water so my mother took off my clothes and threw them in the shit, then began spitting on me so she could wipe the shit off. I was not only covered in shit, but then covered in spit. It was horrible, fucking horrible." Chang pauses dramatically. "I still smell the shit. I still do. That's why I take these baths, you know, because I still smell the shit."

"Chang, when my dad threw me over the Berlin Wall, I got shot by a fucking Cossack. Getting shot is worse than getting shit on you."

"I would take the bullet any day. What do you know of being covered in shit?"

"I know my fucking leg hurt like a bitch," I say.

"It probably did hurt."

"No shit, it fucking did."

We sit there for a long time in silence.

We don't do anything.

Times passes.

We don't know what to say to each other. But we don't expect anything to be said.

We know our lives are boring.

Chang lives in a tiny bedroom living off of SSI checks for post-traumatic stress disorder.

I go to work and sit alone waiting to die.

Our lives do not amount to much.

We are not powerful men.

We are weak little men.

We are so weak, pitiful and catastrophic.

Neither of us has any money in the bank.

We have no property.

People talk about *getting what you want out of life, grabbing life by the balls, sucking the marrow out of bones, going for your dreams, living the life of your dreams, being successful, working hard playing hard, taking advantage of all that is the American Dream.*

The American Dream!

Chang and I have never done those things.

Our lives came, we got them, and sadly we still have them. We endure them.

We have completely avoided the American Dream.

The American Dream requires a lot of ambition.

Between Chang and I, there probably isn't an ounce of ambition.

"Chang, are we dirty commies?"

"I'm in a bathtub and I don't have a job."

"You're right."

"You wash dishes."

"I know."

"Is there anything to live for?"

"I'm not sure. We never get laid."

"No, we don't."

"We suck."

"Nobody wants to fuck us," Chang says.

"You would think after a year of not getting laid your balls would explode and you would die, but you don't. You keep going on, still not getting laid."

"There is global warming and two wars, and we are sitting around talking about not getting laid."

"I'm sure the soldiers in Iraq are thinking about their balls too," I say.

"Balls."

"Balls."

"You're right," Chang says.

"I know, we're in our twenties and we can't get laid. Girls even tell us we're attractive. And we still can't get laid."

"They know about us."

"What about us?"

"They know we're weird."

"They know we don't pine," I say.

"I can't pine. I must bathe. That shit smell never goes away. Maybe girls don't like me because I smell like shit."

"Let's not talk about not getting laid anymore. It depresses me."

"Yes, it's a sad subject."

"Have I told you about my $10,000 bill?"

"No."

"Well, the student loan people sent me a letter saying that since I didn't make any of the payments, now I owe them one installment of $10,000."

"That's wild."

"Yeah, no fucking shit."

"I don't understand, if you couldn't pay small amounts, how do they expect you to pay $10,000 in one installment?"

"I don't fucking know."

"What are you going to do?"

"I don't know."

"You should write a proposal to a video game company."

"Do what?"

"You like video games."

"Yeah, so what?"

"Well, make up a plot for a game and send it to the companies. And they will give you money and probably let you work with them."

"That sounds like a lot of work."

"I don't have any other ideas."

"That's it. Write a video game."

"Yeah."

"About what?"

"I don't know, I'm not the one who owes $10,000."

"You're saying I have to do this myself. This requires some kind of drive, some kind of like motivation."

"You like being in a shithole?"

"No."

"Isn't that motivation?"

"I don't know. I've gotten used to being in a shithole."

"You like living in a shithole?"

"Don't you?"

"Yeah, kind of."

"I should just die," I say.

"No."

"No?"

"If you die, who will sit with me?"

"I don't know. Your mom?"

"My mother spit on me to clean off the shit."

"I'm not very good at doing things that matter."

"The water is getting cold. I'm getting out."

That is the sign for me to leave the bathroom.

I don't know what to do.

It just seems like the world is heavy. That it is like a big cement monster that is crushing me, that is pummeling me with scorpion claws, stinging me, biting me, throwing bricks at my head, slamming cinder blocks on my nuts, eating me alive, showing me that I am worthless, that my life on this planet is a futile little pile of meat that ends in immobility, death, then I'm sent underground with a shitty tombstone that doesn't signify who I was, what I was about. It just states my name, year of birth and day of death. I don't feel lucky at all to be alive.

3.

I'm standing in the dish-tank at work.

The dish-tank is my hole.

There is a giant dishwasher next to me. It is made of metal and makes a lot of noise when dishes are run through it.

The dish-tank area smells like garbage. At night I throw bleach everywhere to try to get some of the smell to go away. But it never does. It always stinks like hell. It makes me stink like hell too.

I'm standing at the dish-tank. Gina brings dishes to it, drops the dishes, and goes back to serving tables.

I watch Gina walk away.

I think, Gina.

Gina has expensive pants and shoes on. She is flashy. She

comes from a world where being flashy is appropriate.

I'm a Russian immigrant working as a dishwasher.

I still think she is cute.

She is half-Greek and half-Irish. She has pretty Greek hair with freckles on her cheeks. I think she is beautiful.

I've had a crush on her since the first day I met her. We got hired together. The manager sat the new hires at a table and I was sitting next to Gina.

I was nervous sitting next to Gina.

I couldn't speak.

I hadn't worked in over a month. I put out fifty applications and no one would hire me. My life at that moment was not going well. I was a pizza boy before but my car broke then I was unemployed. I applied at many places to be things that paid more and required less work. But my life sucks and I could not get any of those jobs. So I applied to the steakhouse as a last resort and became a dishwasher.

I remember sitting next to Gina. She was no more than a foot away from me. I was staring at that pretty face I'm sure with a look of terror on my face and she said, "What did you do last night?"

I said something stupid, like, "I read a book."

I'm not good with people. I should have said that I went out and had lots of fun, with lots of friends, that I'm cool and all kinds of shit like that.

Instead I said, "I read a book."

She knew I was a nerd then. Not only a nerd, but a poor nerd.

I hated myself so much at that moment. I kept thinking that something was wrong with me, that I was like a plague, inept, faulty, defective, that I needed to murder myself in cold blood.

I'm not good with people.

Gina didn't ask me any more questions after that, and I didn't ask her any either. I kept silent during the training process.

That is the story of my life.

I always keep silent.

I like Gina though.

She is really cool.

She is always really nervous and high-strung, pissed off, and says things like, "I hate people."

Gina always has this look of terror mixed with hate on her face. I find that very attractive.

I'm afraid though.

I always think after I say something that it is wrong, that somehow I have fucked up, that the person I'm talking to will hate me.

I'm always convinced that people hate me; it makes for an uncomfortable existence.

And now five months later I'm still standing in the dish-tank, thinking of Gina.

I should win an award for self-destruction, self-mutilation, and self-loathing.

The award will be presented by Tom Cruise. There will be an audience of several million. Tom Cruise will say, "And now, the award for the most self-loathing human alive goes to... Vasily Krymov."

I will walk up on the stage.

The crowd will roar with applause.

Tom Cruise will hand me the award.

I will give my thank you speech: "I would like to thank my father and mother for always showing me that they hated me since I was born. I would like to thank that Cossack for shooting me when I was six, and thank God for forsaking me."

I don't believe in God, but it is always important to thank

God in those types of speeches.

Tom Cruise will stand behind me, chuckling to himself, and he will say under his breath, "Fucking loser."

I will hear him say, "Fucking loser." And think of it as positive reinforcement that I am fucking worthless and should be shot for crimes against those who have ambition and a desire for the Good Life.

Gina walks by and says, "Hey Vasily, want to help me make these salads."

I stand there like an idiot and say, "Sure."

I follow Gina to the cooler where the salad mix is located.

We stand there alone.

She throws the salad mix onto the glass plates and I throw the cheese on.

Dishwashers aren't supposed to help servers make salads, but since it is Gina I do.

Gina knows this.

She is taking advantage of my crush.

I know this.

This is not said out loud.

I do not care that she is taking advantage of my crush. Worse things have happened. I like being around her and she is letting me. She even invited me to be around her. And I like being alone with her, which is even better.

While preparing the salad, Gina asks, "How old are you?"

I don't want to answer.

I'm old.

Not really.

She is twenty-two and I'm twenty-six.

That is a big difference.

Maybe not, but in my head it is.

"I'm twenty-six."

I hate myself for being twenty-six.

She says, "Do you go to school?"

"No."

I stand there in silence.

I don't know what to say.

I'm so afraid, weird, and dysfunctional.

She doesn't know this.

She doesn't know me.

I never talk about myself.

That is my fault.

I go around saying things, but never saying anything about myself. I assume it is because I'm so boring and I know that and don't want anyone else to think I'm boring.

Gina is finished with the salads.

We leave the cooler and she goes back to serving tables and I go back to the dish-tank.

This is my life.

God, I hate myself.

4.

Chang and I are sitting at the Waffle House.

It is around 2:30AM.

We are sitting at the counter reading in silence.

Time passes easily at the Waffle House.

It is a good place to sit when you can't sleep. You eat some food, read some, listen to truckers talk, and let the shit of the universe stay outside the Waffle House.

My favorite server at the Waffle House is Isabella. Isabella is a disaster of a human being. She grew up on the Eastside of Youngstown. Which is a small third-world country located inside of America.

I have a small crush on Isabella. Not as prominent as the crush on Gina, but a crush nonetheless.

Isabella motions for me to go outside and smoke a cigarette with her. She looks emotional so I prepare myself to listen to sentences of misery, hardship, and endless toil that will only end with the cessation of her beating heart.

We are standing outside.

The weather is nice.

There are stars and the moon shines at half crescent.

It is a good moon, a nice bright moon that shines on our bewildered faces, lighting up our wrinkles placed there by years of industrial suffering done in the name of possessing food.

"I left my boyfriend," Isabella says.

"You did?"

I say this trying to sound concerned, like I care. I don't care though; her boyfriend has nothing to do with me. I met him once and he was overweight and had nothing interesting to say.

"Yeah, I did. I just couldn't handle taking care of him anymore. It was starting to get on my nerves. He started getting fat from not working. And all the fucking time he says he's going to get a job and never does. All he does is play video games and smoke weed."

"That sucks."

"Yeah, I know. I've talked to everybody and everybody says I should leave him. I don't know though. I've been with him for years."

She has spoken to everybody; that's typical. People who tell everybody their problems get on my nerves. People view their breakups as theatrical musicals in this country. They need a fucking audience to do anything of significance.

"Do you want to hang out then?" I say.

"Yeah, that sounds good."

"I think we would go well together. We both are like free

spirits and shit." That is such a load of bullshit. We wouldn't go well together.

"Yeah, we should try it," Isabella says.

"When is your next day off?"

"Tomorrow."

"Mine is tomorrow too. We should hang out."

"All right, it's a date."

We go inside.

I'm very happy about this.

I sit down next to Chang. He says, "What happened?"

"We have a date tomorrow."

"Are you sure about this?"

"I'm so alone," I say.

"So am I."

"We're fucked."

"Yes."

"Somebody has to be nice to me someday."

Chang pauses for a second and looks deep into his mind, trying desperately to recall an incident when someone was nice to him. He says, "Vasily, if she doesn't come over, we'll go to the bar and get drunk. How does that sound?"

I look down at my coffee, and say, "Okay."

5.

I'm sitting alone after getting back from the Waffle House.

I can't sleep because of the coffee.

When I can't sleep I watch YouTube videos.

YouTube is better than television.

Television is self-murder.

The television tells you what sounds nice. YouTube tells you what sounds horrible.

I type the phrase "Peak Oil" into the search bar.

A long list of movies appears. I click the first one.

The movie starts.

Thousands of dead bodies are strewn everywhere!

Starving children are murdering dogs with kitchen knives!

Elderly women are sucking dick for saltines!

Thousands are in line to buy water!

Nuclear bombs explode, vaporizing humanity!

The suburbs are ghost towns, their pools full of muck, their decks rotting!

Automobiles are rusted along the side of the road, parked where they ran out of gas!

Poor suburban children are sitting around a fire wearing mittens!

Women cry in the streets!

Men hit each other with clubs!

Asthmatics are coughing to death in their living rooms!

Humans buried in mass graves!

Malaria is killing millions!

Starving families are chewing on bark for nutrition!

Wal-Mart is going bankrupt!

People are eating their pet hamsters!

The pyramid eye of the Illuminati hangs over all of it laughing hysterically!

Total carnage!

Rampant death!

Pestilence!

Evil forces lurk everywhere!

All of humanity dies and nothing is left but their garbage!

I like movies like that.

Peak oil movies are good for that.

Now I search for 'Global Warming.'

A long list pops up. I click on one I haven't seen before.

The movie comes on.

A tidal wave engulfs Manhattan!

Thousands of poets, novelists, painters, movie producers, actors, models, musicians, office workers, and Puerto Rican maids are engulfed in a tidal wave of water. You can hear the screams of dying painters and poets for miles!

Florida is consumed. The elderly and the beautiful are drowned!

Polar bear paws smack the water, and you see them drown!

Penguins are crying in agony!

An ice age begins!

Snow cloaks America!

Millions of dead bodies are covered in ice and snow, frozen solid!

There is no food!

People murder each other for Kit Kats!

It is so cold all the pipes freeze in America at the same exact second and they all break!

All the plumbers have frozen to death and no one is alive to fix the pipes!

The fingers of a small child are black with frostbite, and an old man carrying a Boy Scout knife cuts him up and eats him for what little nutrition he has to offer!

Women and children wearing mittens!

Humans have cut down all the trees for firewood, creating deforestation, which causes mudslides!

Mudslides kill millions!

The pyramid eye of the Illuminati hangs over all of it laughing hysterically!

Total carnage!

Rampant death!

Pestilence!

Evil forces lurk everywhere!

All of humanity dies and nothing is left but their garbage!

Another good movie.

I search '9/11 conspiracy.'

A lot of movies pop up.

I click one.

The movie begins.

A man stands before the camera and says, "Your country has lied to you. You are fucking stupid. Is life a Jerry Bruckheimer film? Buildings don't fall from fire! Those fires couldn't make that steel melt! This is reality! In reality, in this universe, that would never happen! Don't let yourselves be tricked! You are smarter than this! There are no terrorists! There is Bush and his Bushies and the Illuminati and they are trying to take away your rights, your freedoms. And you are giving them up! You are selling your mind and soul to the highest bidder for what? You don't even know! You are Americans!"

The man is screaming this.

Then the man keeps screaming:

"YOU ARE LETTING IT FUCKING HAPPEN!

"YOU ARE LETTING IT FUCKING HAPPEN!

"YOU ARE LETTING IT FUCKING HAPPEN!

"YOU ARE LETTING IT FUCKING HAPPEN!

"YOU ARE LETTING IT FUCKING HAPPEN!

"YOU ARE LETTING IT FUCKING HAPPEN!

"YOU ARE LETTING IT FUCKING HAPPEN!"

This guy is serious.

"The government planned 9/11 and carried it out. You can trust no one. I'm not talking about the government, because there is no government. There is the Illuminati. Secret organizations of Yale graduates that have been working together since the time of Christ to bleed humanity dry of individuality, happiness, and normal human compassion!"

I stop watching YouTube videos, take a shit, and go to sleep.

6.

Sasha and I sit in the Paprika Café.

The Paprika Café serves Hungarian food, which is almost like Russian food. They both involve cabbage.

It is a new restaurant in Youngstown. We like the place. It is small and has a nice atmosphere. It kind of smells like cabbage-hell, but you get used to it after a while.

Sasha has no kids or husband, and doesn't really care about anything. She owns a bar in downtown Youngstown called Sweet Jenny's, after the Bruce Springsteen song.

"Isabella is supposed to come over tonight," I say.

"For real? Good job," Sasha says.

"She won't come," I say.

"Do you care?"

"Of course I care. I want to get laid."

"That's a good point."

"I'm trying not to care though. I'm trying to be strong and think about other things, like video games and washing dishes."

"That sounds like a lot to think about."

"Seriously, do you think she'll come?"

"She's a junkie. Do you have any coke?"

"No," I say.

"Then probably not. Cokeheads date cokeheads. You know the rules." She eats a spoonful of cabbage soup and says, "This is great cabbage."

"It's cabbage. How do you fuck up cabbage?"

"You can fuck up cabbage."

"All cabbage tastes the same."

"Maybe."

"I don't feel like I can live anymore."

"What the hell does that even mean?"

"It means that when I walk around this planet, I keep getting the urge to blow my brains out."

"You don't have a gun."

"You need to take me and my suicide seriously."

"Listen motherfucker, you keep reminding me of Lizaveta. But from Lizaveta I know that people who are going to kill themselves don't sit around and talk about it like sack-asses."

"I know, I'm not going to kill myself."

"No shit. Quit reminding me of Lizaveta," Sasha says.

"Why can't we talk about Lizaveta?"

"Because she's dead."

"What's wrong with dead people? Are we just supposed to forget them now that they are dead? Pretend their lives never occurred?"

"I feel guilty."

"Who doesn't feel guilty? We let her go nuts and die. We watched her disintegrate, we watched her go nuts, we watched like complacent assholes as our sister leaped off the precipice into a pit of jackals, to drown in madness!"

Sasha looks down at her food and says, "That was mean."

A single tear falls from Sasha's left eye.

I say, "We didn't do anything. We watched her die. She's dead."

"What are we supposed to do?"

"I guess nothing. But we could at least mention her once in a while."

"There's no point. If she wanted to be mentioned, she wouldn't have killed herself. You can't shit-talk about the dead unless they are poets or politicians. Shit-talking dead people who aren't famous doesn't seem right."

"No, it doesn't," I say.

"Sometimes I dream about her. She doesn't talk in the dreams. She doesn't look at me either. I don't want her to look at me. If Lizaveta ever looked at me in one of my dreams, I would wake to kill myself. I couldn't even look at her toward the end. She was ruined. I couldn't look at her ruins. It didn't make me feel better. Usually I feel somewhat better when someone is doing worse than me. But that was *too* worse."

"I didn't really know her."

"I did. She was all right. I remember playing in the yard a lot when we were little and doing shit like that. But you know how high school is. Everyone goes their own way. Everyone thinks they are awesome and has to be cool."

"I got laid more in high school."

"It is hard to get laid after you're twenty-two. People start to think they *must* get married, have babies, shit like that. It is like a gun is pointed at their head or something."

"It's strange," I say. "You go through high school and the next four years randomly fucking people, and then when twenty-two hits, it's like, 'I gotta get married and have babies.' When I think about most people's lives, I see it as being made up of a series of escapes. They face reality and escape. They face it again and escape, and face it and escape, then die."

7.

Isabella is supposed to call around nine o'clock.

It is 8:49PM.

That's eleven minutes.

I'm freaking out.

I cleaned the house.

I vacuumed the floor, did the dishes, took the garbage out, even dusted.

The place looks good.

I'm sitting in front of the computer, improving my MySpace page, trying to waste time, trying to make time go easier.

Time won't go easy.

Time is crushing me.

It is 8:50PM.

A minute has passed.

I'm still sitting here.

I wish she would call early.

She won't call.

Isabella hates me.

No, she doesn't hate me.

She doesn't care about me.

She views me as someone who sits at the Waffle House all night reading with a strange man, looking terrified, never saying the right thing, unable to hold a decent conversation.

She always goes, "What's up, Vasily?"

And like a fuckhead I say, "Nothing."

Then she says with that inflection that signifies she is speaking to a loser, "You live an interesting life."

But what am I supposed to say? Am I supposed to describe how I watched global warming disaster videos for four hours last night? Am I supposed to describe how Gina makes my heart swoon, my cheeks redden, and I get all stupid when I'm around her. I can't say that to Isabella, because I'm trying to fuck her. Talking about how my mother hates me is not how to get chicks. I can't describe how I lay in bed for two hours dwelling on how big of a fucking ass I am, how I'm a failure, how I'm crushed by history, fucked, lonely, and want to die.

No, I can't say those things out loud.

To get a chick you have to say something witty, you have to get them to laugh, you have to put on a performance, be a comedian.

I can't make jokes.

My sense of humor is deadpan.

Deadpan doesn't get the bitches.

It is 8:52PM.

She isn't going to call.

Maybe she will.

She won't.

Maybe she will.

I don't know.

My life is horrible.

My mind keeps racing to horrible conclusions. I'm a complete waste and need to be vanquished before a live studio audience.

I go to my room and lie on my bed.

I don't turn on music.

It is quiet.

I lie in the fetal position.

My eyes are closed.

I don't cry.

I feel like it would be therapeutic.

But I'm a man and men don't cry.

When I was younger, it was easier for me to get girls.

When I was young I was cool, I was an artsy kid. All the kids were artsy kids. We were artsy kids and we hung out at certain bars and we met, got drunk, had sex.

Now those artsy kids have babies, and instead of being artsy kids, they are moms and dads and have jobs that require education, like hairdressing and teaching middle-school. Some became addicts, but they also became moms and dads.

I have no kids.

They all tell me, "Vasily, get some kids, get married. Why didn't you get married to Jessica?"

I answer: "Because she sucks."

No one believes me though. Everyone thinks I'm immature and an asshole for not marrying Jessica and having loads of offspring even though Jessica and I fought all the time.

It is 8:55PM.

She isn't going to call.

I need to die.

Maybe if I lay here in this dark room in silence I'll fall asleep, and if I'm really lucky I'll have an aneurysm.

That won't happen.

I'll wake up knowing I was stood up.

I remember when I was younger, I was with this girl and we fucked all night, and the sun came up, it shone through the windows, and she looked so pretty.

Those days are gone.

It isn't cool to be weird when you get older.

Being weird is cool when you're twenty, but as time passes you get creepy.

I'm creepy now.

And that's why Isabella isn't calling.

And that's why she won't come.

I'm such a failure.

If I had some drugs she'd be here.

I have no drugs.

Drugs make me depressed, scared, and lonely.

I already feel depressed, scared, and lonely.

I don't need anything that will exacerbate those emotions.

I lie here for a moment and try not to exist.

I remain perfectly still.

Like a rock or cactus.

It doesn't work, I still exist!

This is bad.

It is 8:59PM.

She won't call.

I'm doomed.

Life is a horrible monstrosity!

I've been stood up before, I can take this.

Now I'm telling myself things, to make myself feel that I'm strong or that I know things, and since I know things I won't let them affect me.

It still makes me want to scream, break my arms and legs and cut myself in a masochistic rampage.

You can't make the truth of your failure go away.

Even if you know every little thing about something, even if you know and understand every calculation, have every bit of news on the subject, even if you can name all the conspirators, have a list of times and dates, study every psychological discipline ever invented, and know exactly who to blame and who not to blame.

It doesn't matter!

It still crushes you.

And here I am crushed.

It's 9:00PM.

What did I do to deserve this?

Nothing.

It isn't a question of deserve.

Isabella likes to feel special.

I know this.

I have this information.

Months ago she said to me, "I like to feel special."

Everybody likes to feel special.

Everyone is running around trying to get other people to make them feel special.

I made her feel special because I asked her out.

She got what she wanted.

She wanted to feel special and I gave her the medicine.

But now she won't come.

I wonder when I first came out of my mother's cunt, back in Russia, if anyone standing there, maybe even the doctor or a nurse, thought, 'One day this man will be stood up and life will crush him.'

Someone had to think it.

Someone should have told me when I was little, "Vasily, everyone is playing a game in life. Everyone is trying to feel special. And to accomplish this, they will hurt you, and you will even hurt people to gain this feeling of power over the world. This is the game that humanity plays."

But that wouldn't have mattered.

Because I would have done it anyway. I would have asked her out anyway. I would have put myself in a position to be humiliated and mutilated before a live studio audience.

Time passes and she does not call, so I call Chang.

"Chang."

"She didn't come?"

"No."

"Bitch!"

"Thanks. To the bar?"

"To the bar."

8.

Chang and I are sitting in Sweet Jenny's.

Sasha is behind the bar serving drinks.

There aren't many people in the bar.

Chang and I sit there like two useless assholes drinking draft beer.

Chang says, "Fucking bitch."

"Yes, a horrible fucking bitch."

Chang is a good friend. Good friends always hate the people who stand up their friends.

Sasha comes over. "You got stood up?"

"Yes."

"Stupid bitch."

"Yes, stupid bitch."

"We should find her and cut her legs off."

"That would accomplish nothing. My penis would still be lonely."

"A lonely penis cries in the rain," Chang says.

"*When we kissed goodbye and parted, I knew we'd never meet again,*" Sasha says, laughing.

"Please don't turn my penis into a Willie Nelson song," I say.

"*Vasily's penis is a dying ember, and only memories remain, and through the ages I'll remember, Vasily's lonely penis crying in the rain,*" Chang sings.

"I should kill both of you," I say.

Sasha and Chang laugh hysterically about my lonely penis. I lower my head in shame.

Sasha says, "What about Gina? You talk about Gina all the time."

"I know, but Gina has such expensive shoes. Her Nikes daunt me."

"She has Nikes?" Chang says.

"Yeah, Nikes," I say.

"Nikes are really expensive," Chang says.

"They are those Nikes with the air shock system thingy," I say.

"You wear ADIDAS," Chang says.

"Yeah, ADIDAS are almost like Nikes," Sasha says.

"Yeah, but my ADIDAS were bought from a discount outlet store for twenty dollars. Her shoes were bought at the mall."

"The mall, that's serious shit," Sasha says.

"The mall, where old people power walk?" Chang says.

"Yeah, the fucking mall. She's a mall person," I say with terror.

"Sometimes when things are on sale, I can get things at the mall," Sasha says.

"The Nikes Gina wears are like brand new. She like, went in there, and was like, 'Give me those hundred-and-twenty dollar pair of Nikes.'"

"Is she rich or something?" Chang says.

"I don't know. She lives in Cortland. Her parents might be school teachers or engineers at the Chevy plant."

"Cortland," Chang says.

"Cortland," Sasha says.

"We live in Youngtown and own ADIDAS."

"We are a sorry bunch," Chang says.

"Is that why you asked Isabella out, because she's poor?" Sasha says.

"Yeah, I guess. I'm a dishwasher. It makes sense for dishwashers to date Waffle House servers, not girls who wear brand new Nikes."

"Yeah, I guess it does. But Isabella never graduated high school and you have junior year credits in Political Science," Sasha says.

"I know, I fucking know. But I didn't graduate. I dropped out and became a dishwasher."

"I guess you're fucked then," Sasha says.

"Get me a Captain and Coke. I need to get drunk."

Sasha pours a Captain and Coke and hands it to me. I take the small straw, stir it around, and throw the straw on the bar and drink.

While gulping the drink, a song comes on. "Strawberry Wine" by Deana Carter.

Everyone becomes quiet.

During the chorus, me, Chang, Sasha, and everybody else in the bar sing along.

When the song ends, a menacing silence encompasses the bar.
Sasha picks up an empty glass and flings it at the wall!
It shatters!
No one even mentions it.

9.

It's Saturday.

The busiest day at the steakhouse.

I hate Saturday.

It'll be like Wednesday and I'll lie in bed and think, Saturday is coming, it'll kill me.

I dread Saturday.

I have fifteen minutes till I have to start so I'm standing at the bar being useless.

Beth, an attractive twenty-two-year-old with a two-year-old daughter, walks up to me and says, "You have that belt on."

I'm wearing a robin-egg blue belt. It holds up my pants.

"Yeah, so."

"People are talking."

The phrase, 'Hell is other people' zips into my brain as I say, "What are people saying?"

I feel like I'm playing some deranged game, because this conversation is so predictable I could kill myself.

"They are saying you might be gay."

"Gay?"

"Yeah, gay."

"Is there anything wrong with being gay?"

She looks confused and says, "Hmm, no."

"Then I'm okay."

"Are you gay?"

"Do you mean I take it up the ass from men?"

"Yes, do you do that?"

"No."

"I didn't think so."

"I have hemorrhoids. I would bleed horribly."

"You're weird, Vasily."

"So are you, Beth."

Beth walks away.

I'm sitting on a milk crate outside before I have to start.

Larry is there.

Larry is a crackhead.

Larry is five-foot-five, 130 pounds, has bad skin and spits a lot.

He has worked at the steakhouse for five years and makes $7.50 an hour.

The boss hates him.

Once the boss screamed, "Larry, if you want to leave, you can go."

Larry stayed.

Larry knows the boss hates him and it pisses her off more that he stays.

The boss won't fire Larry because she knows he wouldn't get a job and would collect unemployment and smoke crack with it.

Larry says to me, "You got any metal?"

"Metal?"

"Yeah, metal, for scrap."

"You scrap shit?"

"Yeah, that's what I do to make extra money. I scrap shit. I go into abandoned houses in Youngstown and take the copper pipes. I get $2.60 a pound for copper."

I don't believe he gets $2.60 a pound for copper, but I don't care anyway.

"I got some stoves in the garage."

"How much do you think they weigh?"

"I have no idea how much the stoves weigh."

"Probably like two-hundred pounds."

"Yeah, probably."

I start work.

There are a million dishes to wash.

They are stacked up three feet high.

I'm not daunted.

I'm the uber-dishwasher.

Diego Jones, an older black cook who used to be a crack-head, runs over to me and says, "I need ramekins."

Everybody always needs ramekins.

I throw the ramekins in.

I start to contemplate suicide.

There are large knives everywhere.

I could grab one and plunge it into my stomach.

Say something really profound like, "I hate Saturdays."

Then die.

I go out to smoke again.

Crazy Dennis is there.

Dennis looks like a man.

But tells people he is a woman.

Dennis does have small tits though, and a bulging ass.

Dennis tells people that he was once a woman, that he got into a car wreck and had to go on steroids, and the steroids made him into, in his words, 'a morphidite.' (Which always makes me think of *Mighty Morphin Power Rangers*.) I always imagine Dennis morphing into a robotic tiger when he speaks.

Dennis also says he was in the army and a Green Beret, once a mechanic, once a trucker, and even at one point a belly dancer.

As we smoke on milk crates, Dennis says to me, "They won't give me a black hat."

The managers gave all the cooks that have been here for at least six months black hats, but they didn't give one to him because he has only been working here for five months, and they don't like him because he's lazy and insane.

Dennis keeps talking. "They won't give me a black hat. I've worked for this company for three years. I mean it was down south where I worked. But I was transferred here. I have seniority over most of these cooks. The managers don't understand how important I am to this business. If I left, half their customers would leave."

"They didn't give me a black hat either," I say.

"You've only been here four months."

"Yeah."

"I've been working for this company for four years. I should get a black hat. Instead I'm walking around with this dirty blue one. I have the mind to just walk out of here. Then they would know how important I am to this business."

"Those bastards," I say earnestly.

"Yeah, those bastards. Why won't they give me a black hat? I show up to work on time. I put in my hours. I work hard here and they won't give me a black hat. Even fucking Larry got a black hat, and he's a crackhead."

"Larry's been here for five years."

"That don't mean shit. He's still a crackhead."

"My cigarette is done. Gotta go."

I'm back at the dish-tank.

The dishes keep coming.

The host, Jeremy, comes up to me.

Jeremy is seventeen and still in high school.

He just spent two days in a juvenile detention center for breaking his stepdad's jaw.

"Jeremy, how was the pen?" I say.

"It was boring. I feel really bad."

"For what? I thought you said he was an asshole."

"He is, but I'm totally not like violent."

"Who cares? Violence is awesome."

"No man, I feel bad. I don't feel good about it."

"No, it's cool. Beating up your parents is awesome!"

"Dude, but like."

"No, don't worry. Life is awesome. 'Beat your parents,' that's what I always say."

Jeremy realizes he's getting fucked-up advice that totally contradicts everything everybody has been telling him for the past week, so he leaves.

I'm walking around.

Gina comes up from behind me and says, "I like your belt."

"Thanks."

"And I can see your underwear," she says, giggling.

I go over to the dish-tank and pull my pants up.

I wonder if that means she likes me.

She likes looking at my underwear.

Why didn't I think of something witty to say like, 'Oh yeah, wanna see the rest of them?'

Or, 'You wanna see what's underneath?'

Or, 'You like looking at my ass?'

But no.

I say nothing.

I get nervous and go over to the dish-tank and pull my pants up.

I'm such an ass.

Why can't I do anything right when it comes to girls?

Especially Gina.

I should blow my brains out.

I'm standing at the dish-tank.

Beth comes over and says, "You going out tonight?"

"No, I don't drink on Saturdays."

"What the hell does that mean, 'I don't drink on Saturdays.' Everybody drinks on Saturdays."

"That's exactly why. The bar will be full of assholes yelling stupid shit at each other. I start to hyperventilate around a lot of people."

"You are so fucking weird. What about tomorrow night? Sunday is quiz night."

"Yeah, tomorrow sounds fine. The bar will be what, half-full. I can handle half-full. I can't handle full."

"Yes Vasily, the bar will only be half-full."

Beth runs away then.

Everybody always invites me to go out. I don't know why. I think they feel sorry for me.

They probably feel sorry for me because I stand here looking morbid all day while washing dishes. But I really don't know how I'm supposed to get into the spirit of washing dishes, like it wouldn't make sense if the dishwasher was giggling and smiling and loving life all day.

Dishwashing sucks.

I'm not a happy dishwasher.

I'm not even a happy person.

On my days off I'm usually completely miserable.

I wonder if Gina is going tomorrow.

I wash dishes, waiting for Gina to drop off some plates.

Gina always asks me to go to the bar, not with her specifically, but she does say things like, "Hey Vasily, you should come out tonight."

But Gina has a boyfriend and I'm always afraid he'll be there, so I never go.

Gina drops off some plates.

I yell, "Hey Gina!"

Gina says, "Hey Vasily!"

"Gina, are you going to the bar tomorrow?"

"Yeah, why? Are you finally going to go out with us?"

"Yeah, I think I might."

A smile comes over her face.

A smile.

Gina has such a pretty smile.

She smiled because of me.

I'm such an ass.

Gina says, "Yeah, and my boyfriend isn't coming. He wants me to act reserved, but I want to have fun tomorrow night."

"That sounds great."

Gina goes back to work.

It is the end of the night.

I walk out into the dining room to bring glasses to the bar.

The female servers are all standing around in a circle.

One server is talking about how her mom doesn't like her boyfriend.

One server is talking about how her boyfriend is going to school to become an electrician.

One server is having a text message war with her boyfriend.

One server is complaining about her boyfriend in bed.

One server is talking about how great the movie *Wild Hogs* is.

I'm sitting outside smoking a cigarette.

It is dark now.

The moon shines a nice light over the mall parking lot.

A seventeen-year-old hostess named Christa is standing near me.

She is obviously anorexic.

She is five-four and weighs eighty-seven pounds.

Without looking at her, I say, "You need to gain weight."

"What?"

"You need to gain weight. Peak oil is coming."

"What the fuck is peak oil?"

"It would take too long to explain. But you need body fat to survive it."

"Isn't oil like something that comes from the ground?"

"Yes, that is correct," I say.

"How does it peak?"

"Listen, it would take too long to explain. All you need to know is that your anorexia is bullshit. You need to gain weight and get fatter. Your head is huge."

She looks at me like I'm an ass, then she leaves.

The night is finally over.

It was a horrible night.

I should have killed myself during it.

But I'm a coward.

I get into my 1990 Jetta.

I sit down and start the car and reach over to turn on the radio.

My hand finds empty space.

I look to where the radio should be.

Nothing is there but a bunch of dangling wires.

I consider punching the steering wheel.

But I don't.

The car has no heat, two of the doors won't open, it burns oil, the horn doesn't work, and now it has no radio.

I consider getting angry but I just finished work and I don't have the energy to dwell on a stupid stereo.

I drive home in silence.

I open the window and let the sound of crickets and frogs flood the car.

The crickets and frogs sound better than most songs anyway.

10.

Chang and I are sitting at the Lampost Lounge.

The Lampost Lounge is the strip joint down the street from where we live.

It is small and weird.

It only ever has about three girls at once.

It is not a classy strip joint.

The Lampost Lounge is a small place that serves alcohol and has three girls in bikinis who will dance on your lap for five dollars.

I told Beth I didn't go to bars on Saturdays. But the Lampost Lounge isn't a bar; it's a small strip joint with never more than ten customers.

Viper, our favorite dancer, comes over and says, "Look who

it is. The dynamic duo of self-flagellation."

Chang looks at me and says, "Is she talking about us?"

Viper says, "Have you two done anything fun lately?"

"No," I say.

"Last week I had an abortion. It was awesome. They got this vacuum cleaner thingy and sucked that little fucker right out."

"They should do that with my brain," Chang says.

"That would be good for America," I say.

"Do either of you fine gentlemen want a dance?"

"Yes, please. I need a dance. The loneliness has consumed me. My heart has been crushed by government policies. My head aches with despair, alienation, desolation, and I can no longer be confronted with this dismal reality without the feel of your butt smashing hard into my genitals. My sad, forsaken, forlorn genitals. My genitals beseech your buttocks, Viper."

Viper looks at me and laughs and says, "Let my ass soothe your genitals. Let my buttocks engulf your discontented member in this neon-lighted tavern of abject misery. Let your postmodern tears plummet to my round white butt cheeks. Allow my ass lumps to soften your burden of being a disgruntled dishwasher, of being a man who feels homeless and weary. Who vomits at the very idea of John Travolta making another movie."

Chang says, "She's good, give her a big tip."

After the dance, Viper leaves.

A dancer named Kathy comes over and says to Chang, "Hey Chang, what's the capitol of Thailand?"

Chang looks confused and says, "Bangkok."

"That's right, Bangkok." As Kathy says this she punches Chang in the dick.

Chang grabs his crotch.

We all laugh at Chang.

Holding his dick, Chang says, "You bitch, I'll kill you."

"You ain't killing shit, Chang," Kathy says.

Then Kathy walks away, laughing.

"She punched you in the dick."

"Life is hopeless."

"I know, but at least we don't tell ourselves that it's awesome and we deserve great things like success and well-mannered children."

"If I owned a gun I would shoot myself."

"You probably would," I say.

Janisa walks over. She's a pretty Puerto Rican girl who speaks Spanish and has an accent, but is actually from Chicago and has never stepped foot in Puerto Rico.

Janisa sits next to Chang and says, "How you doing?"

"Kathy just punched me in the dick."

"Oh yeah? Do you need a massage?"

"With your hand?"

"Yeah, not inside of course." Janisa moves her mouth close to Chang's ear and says, "There's something about Asians that gets me wild."

Chang smiles like a little boy.

"Please," Chang says.

"Ten dollars."

"Okay."

Chang puts ten dollars in her garter belt.

Janisa massages Chang's bruised penis.

Chang says, "I'm an immigrant too."

"I'm from Chicago, but where you from?"

"China. You know what the Long March is?"

"No, what's that?"

"If you want you can come back to my place and I'll show

you," Chang says, so suave.

Janisa laughs hysterically.

Chang looks at me and says, "This bitch is all about me."

I look straight ahead and say, "You made her laugh. That's the first step to the removal of panties."

Chang whispers to Janisa, "Your eyes, your voice, your arms, your very essence makes me crumble. I collapse like the Twin Towers when I'm in your presence. My cock swells, throbs. I need, I need to impale you with my cock. My hard cock is reaching out to you, trying to become friends with your vagina."

"You is crazy," Janisa says, laughing.

"Yeah baby."

Janisa finishes her penis massage and walks away.

I say to Chang, "You're more socially inept than I am."

"I'm on SSI. I can do anything I want."

"True. I'm a dishwasher. There are regulations I have to follow."

"Yes, you must remain decent at all times. You must always put on a good pose so as not to tarnish the good name of your employer. I, on the other hand, am employed by The People. They employ me to be crazy, to sit alone in my little cell. Society needs people like me to look down on. They need me so there is always a definition of what crazy is. I am paid to keep a line between insanity and what is called sane. My insanity, even if it be only thinking I smell like shit all the time, allows people who think that buying a Hummer will make them happy to convince themselves that they're sane. There are lines that must be drawn. Buying a Hummer equals happiness, getting Road Runner even though it is only a split second faster than DSL equals happiness, owning Nikes and not ADIDAS equals happiness, buying brand names is better than buying generic and it all equals happiness. See

Vasily, that's why they give me money, because I am a line, I symbolize insanity. Personally, I don't think I'm insane. But they do. They have convinced themselves that I am beyond help, that I am mentally fucked. That I deserve a free small apartment, a food card, and spending money because they consider me insane. People, when they sign their name to take out a thirty year mortgage on a shitty stupid house in a so-called nice neighborhood, can think, 'This might be insane, but at least I'm not Chang who thinks he smells like shit all the time.'"

"Are you planning on staying on SSI until you're dead or something?"

"Yes, I refuse to go back. I feel ashamed, so ashamed, humiliated, I feel like I'm being ravaged by nonsense. The last time I had a job this girl said to me, 'Have you heard that new song by Avril Lavigne?' I stood there terrified. I did hear the song one night in the car. I couldn't understand how parents would let their children listen to that shit. I would rather have my kids watch hardcore porn than listen to Avril Lavigne." Chang yells so the whole bar can hear him, "I fucking hate Avril Lavigne!"

A random guy in his twenties yells, "So do I! That bitch is stupid!"

"Damn straight!" Chang says.

I yell to the bartender, "Hey, I'm buying this man a shot and then we're going."

The bartender brings over a shot of chilled Yukon Jack.

Chang throws it back and we leave.

11.

I wake up on Sunday morning.

There is crying coming from the bathroom.

I walk to the door and see Sasha crying.

Sasha cries a lot.

"What's wrong?"

"Nothing."

Sasha always responds 'nothing.'

"Sasha, I'm serious. You're crying like a motherfucker in here."

"Sometimes when I look in the mirror, I see her. I look like her, you know. And there she is, Lizaveta, staring at me from my own face."

"You do look like her."

"I know asshole, that's what I'm trying to say. I look like her."

"You know I have to look at you, and I see her. You laugh like her. You even stick your tongue out like her when you're happy."

Sasha sits there, holding her face, and says, "It is strange when people die; it announces your death also. It marks everyone. It puts into your pocket a little black rock that you carry around symbolizing that you will die one day. I never really knew anyone who died. We left Russia and had no friends here. Our grandparents are dead, but we left them when we were little and never got to know them. So I had not been marked by death. Now I am marked. You realize what death is when someone close dies. You realize it because you think of them all the time. 'I want to call Lizaveta,' I think, and realize Lizaveta is dead. Buying presents at Christmas, I think, 'Lizaveta would love this,' and then realize Lizaveta is dead. It is Lizaveta's birthday and I remember I have to get a card for Lizaveta, and then I realize I don't have to because Lizaveta is dead. And then I realize that one day I will die, and someone will think, 'Sasha's birthday is coming up, I need to get her a card. Oh wait, she's dead.' It means I'm not there. Lizaveta is not here. She just isn't here. Lizaveta stopped moving, her heart ceased to beat, and we've put her underground in a box. Lizaveta no longer participates in the lives of people. That will be me one day, a person who no longer participates in the lives of people. The world will go on without me." She wipes her eyes and cheeks with toilet paper. "Ever see those old graves with the Civil War emblems on them?"

"Yeah."

"Those graves are so old, no one even puts flowers there anymore. Those men have been dead for over a hundred years. When I go to Lizaveta's grave, I look at them. Those old tombstones, I read the names on them without wondering who they were, because I know I can never know. But I wonder about myself. Here, now, I am living. I am on this planet and every day I wake up to go to work in order to pay bills, to take care of things, and even try to suck some happiness from the day. But a hundred and fifty years from now everyone I know will be dead. No one will think, 'Where is Sasha? What's Sasha up to? I wonder how Sasha is doing?' No one, not one living person. Even if I have kids, my great-great-great grandchildren will not remember me. Perhaps they might research their ancestors one day, but I won't be anything but a name on a family tree. They will stare at my name and point at the name 'Sasha Krymov' and no emotion will spring into them. It will just be silence; because one day, I will be condemned to be silenced."

"Sasha?"

"What?"

"I don't need this shit when I first wake up in the morning."

"You need this shit all fucking day!"

"I'm going to check my email."

"Whatever."

12.

I'm outside the bar sitting in my car.

 People I work with are inside.

 They invited me here.

 I am welcome.

 They probably feel bad for me.

 I know they do, everyone feels bad for me.

 No, that's not true.

 No one feels bad for anyone else.

 Everyone is a monster raping the earth.

 Gina and Beth are in there.

 I would like to have sex with either of them.

 They both have boyfriends.

 So it doesn't matter.

So why am I going in?

I don't know.

I never do things like this.

I never hang out with co-workers.

Hanging out with co-workers is a sign of getting old or dying.

I'm not dying; I'm just going to a bar.

My life is obsolete to theirs.

They are all going to nursing schools.

I'm not going to any school.

Gina wears Nikes.

I wear ADIDAS.

I have no life.

Neither do they, but they have convinced themselves they do.

And that's the difference between them and me.

But that doesn't matter.

Because with a proper amount of alcohol they won't notice that I'm a stumble-bum who has failed at being human.

I'm human.

That's true.

Crackhead Larry doesn't think about shit like this.

He's a lot better at poverty than me. He knows that getting scrap metal will get him cigarettes and crack.

I don't know these things.

I'm giving my scrap metal away for free.

He knows it's dumb to hang out with co-workers who wear Nikes.

I don't.

I'm sitting here thinking it is a great idea.

This is a bad idea.

Everyone in there terrifies me.

It can't be that bad.

They are just people.

I can't be so terrified all the time.

I must open the car door and walk to the door of the bar and be a human being.

I wore a nice shirt, I'm presentable.

I got the shirt two years ago at Christmas from my parents.

Everyone looks down on me.

They invited me so they could look down on me.

Because they are all snobs.

I hate them.

No, I don't.

They've never done anything to me.

There's no reason to hate them.

They are just people.

They walk around and worry about things.

We have a lot in common. We worry.

I get out of the car.

I'm walking to the door.

It is terrifying.

I wish I would have a seizure right now.

A seizure would be good.

It would be a good excuse for not showing up at a bar.

'Why didn't you come?'

'I got there but I had a seizure in the parking lot.'

'Oh Vasily, I'm so sorry.'

That would be a great excuse.

But I'm not going to have a seizure because I'm not epileptic.

I'm actually in very good health.

I enter the bar.

There are people everywhere.

Not as crowded as a Friday or Saturday.

But still a lot of fucking people.

Someone is yelling "Vasily!" at me.

I look over. It's Beth and Gina.

At least two people like me.

Beth is sitting with her boyfriend.

Gina is sitting by herself, drinking a Long Island Iced Tea. She keeps hand-dancing like a raver.

I wish Chang or Sasha were here. Without them I feel defenseless against the masses.

I wave my hand, go to get a drink.

It takes like ten minutes because there are a bunch of assholes standing around the bar.

I get a drink.

I sit down at the table.

Beth says, "So what's up?"

"I'm excited to be at the bar."

"It's quiz night!"

"Yeah, I'm pumped."

I have no idea what to say.

I sit next to Gina.

Gina is severely drunk.

She keeps touching me, which makes me happy I chose to come.

It is also karaoke night.

One of my co-workers, Diamond, goes up and sings some emo song I've never heard and never want to hear again.

Everyone claps.

Some guy with a mullet is putting on quiz night.

He tells everyone to list as many movies as possible that John Travolta was in.

John Travolta.

Sometimes I wish I was back in Russia eating cabbage in Siberia.

I start to panic about all this John Travolta excitement and start drinking rum and Cokes.

Life is getting better now.

I start dancing with Diamond.

I'm not even sure who Diamond is.

She never speaks to me.

She's a bartender at the steakhouse.

She looks really weird.

I know she has two kids and lives in the ghetto of Warren.

And she says she is twenty-six, which is the same age as me.

She is my age but I feel no relation to her.

She even looks quite a bit older than me.

Diamond and I dance.

I can't dance.

I'm tone-deaf and have no rhythm.

It is going badly.

Someone sings a ska song so I skank.

Everyone starts staring at me.

They are wondering what I'm doing.

Nobody knows.

They are confused about my skanking.

I am a joke.

Humanity hates me.

The song is over.

Then "Inside Out" by Eve 6 comes on. Diamond is my age, so she is a late 90s douchebag like me.

Diamond and I drunkenly scream the song at each other.

We both find *faith in nothing*.

Faith in nothing does not unify unless you're drunk.

Faith in nothing does not create revolutions or unionize the masses.

It creates a good profit margin for bars, liquor stores, and drug dealers.

I sit down next to Gina.

Gina is so drunk she can't even talk.

I feel like I'm floating in a spaceship.

There is nobody here that I really know or can relate to.

Nobody here even really knows who I am.

I don't really know who anybody else is either.

I feel like I have no identity and they have no identities.

It is kind of nice, this drunken spaceship.

Beth gets into a fight with her boyfriend.

They are having text message wars.

They are sitting next to each other though.

Text messages cost a dime.

They have spent like thirty dollars to fight each other in the last ten minutes.

I don't know why they don't just talk.

I'm not even sure what they're fighting about.

I ask Beth, "What the fuck are you two fighting about?"

"As a joke I wrote, 'I hate you,' in a text message and now he thinks I'm mad at him."

"That's stupid."

"I know."

She knows it is stupid but she is participating in the argument anyway. Their whole relationship is like that. They see each other for one day and fight, which means they have a huge text message war. Then for two days they don't speak, then they have a text message war to make up. It is insane. They seem to enjoy these pseudo-fights. These breakups and make-ups. Like it is part of having a normal relationship.

I really start to drink.

I get drunker and drunker.

I feel stupid for even coming.

I just fucking feel stupid and drunk.

I look around and Beth is gone. Supposedly she is fighting with her boyfriend outside now.

Gina is drunk and everyone is asking her if she needs a ride home. This makes Gina happy. It makes Gina feel like people care about her.

Then I'm sitting in my car, driving home.

Regretting that I ever went.

I'm happy that it was fun.

But when you're drunk and no one is in the car with you, driving home from the bar is fucking sad.

I should unstrap my seatbelt.

Slam down on the pedal.

Look out the window at the moon one more time.

And then slam the car into a rail.

Oh that would be nice.

I don't slam into a rail.

I don't do anything but start crying.

I feel so lonely.

People were not meant to feel this lonely.

People are pack animals.

I'm so alone.

When I'm with people.

They seem not like me.

Chang and Sasha are there.

But they only help so much.

I'm still the one who has to decide what I must direct my body to do.

I'm always responsible.

Others, they don't mind letting some person tell them what to do, they don't mind some old book dictating their actions and beliefs.

I don't know, but I never could.

I'm alone.

Alone on the highway, heading to the Waffle House, not because I need or even like Waffle House eggs. I have eggs at my house. But I don't want to go home and sit alone. I can't do it.

I'm so drunk.

I'm so lonely.

I'm so afraid.

I was shot going over the Berlin Wall for the American Dream. But all I got was drunk.

And very very lonely.

I pull into the Waffle House parking lot.

I'm sitting in my car, looking through the Waffle House window. Isabella walks around in her server uniform, looking young and pretty. Looking so beautiful to my drunk eyes.

Isabella stood me up.

She left me to die.

I don't care.

I go in.

Isabella actually smiles when she sees me.

I sit down and say, "I'm fucking drunk."

Isabella says, "I'm sorry about the other day."

"I didn't expect you to show up," I say.

"I woke up late and didn't have time to call you."

"I'm drunk."

"Where'd you get drunk?"

"At a bar in Warren."

"Want anything to eat?"

"Yeah, a sausage egg and cheese on a burger bun."

"Okay."

I can't hate Isabella.

I can't hate her, but the Waffle House isn't helping my state of mind.

I'm sitting here in silence.

Everyone knows that Isabella stood me up.

She has told everyone and they made fun of me before I came in.

This is life. You do something stupid and the world gives you the gift of humiliation.

After I'm done eating, Isabella invites me to go outside to smoke with her.

I'm so drunk and needy I accept.

We stand with a nice breeze hitting us.

Isabella says, "I think I've really figured myself out."

"Yeah?"

"Yeah, I think I've got a new aura about me. I read my horoscope today and it said that good things were going to happen."

"Is that true?"

"Yeah, I said to my boyfriend, 'You get a job or get the hell out of my life.' And he didn't get a job, so I told him, 'Good riddance.' And I feel a lot happier."

"That's really good."

"So what's going on with you?"

"I got drunk."

"Yeah, anything else?"

"No," I say, "but I'm pretty happy about being drunk for the moment."

"That's good."

We finish our cigarettes and go inside.

I think I've really figured myself out. I think I've got a new aura about me.

Her words pierce my drunken brain.

I feel so bad for humanity I could scream.

I do not scream. I just feel horrible.

I think I've really figured myself out. I think I've got a new aura about me.

What does that even mean?

How does figuring yourself out lead to a new aura?

People are really fucked up.

This is the world I live in.

I'm in hell.

I'm drunk and I'm in hell.

This is how it always ends when I get drunk. I'm happy and dancing and eventually someone says something like, "I think I've really figured myself out. I think I've got a new aura about me," and it all goes to hell.

I get up to leave and Isabella says to me, "So where you going?"

I think about saying that I'm going home to kill myself because she is so tragically fucked that it saddens me to the point of suicide, but instead I say, "Home."

13.

I'm at my parents' house to pick up letters.

Some letters from bill companies still come to their house.

Usually if I go there my mother tries to make me feel guilty for being born, then gives me a twenty dollar bill.

I'm sitting at the kitchen table, drinking coffee, staring around the kitchen.

My mother sits on the other side of the table and says to me in Russian, "Your father is brooding."

"Yeah?"

"He won't tell me why. He just broods."

"Oh yeah?"

"Yeah, he won't talk to me. He goes to work and then comes home, makes himself a sandwich and immediately goes outside and does yard work."

"The yard looks nice."

"Do you think your father is brooding?"

"What?"

"Do you think your father is brooding?"

"I don't know. I haven't seen him in weeks."

"He won't tell me."

"You've been married for thirty years, your lives are like an assembly line producing boredom and shit."

"Our lives are great. We are middle-class. Look at this house. We live in Vienna, not Youngstown. We are good solid Americans. We even have citizenship."

"This place takes everything human about a human and turns it into a Subway Special."

"We worked hard to get you to this country. You need to respect me and be thankful for all that I've done for you."

"I remember being little and picking mushrooms in the forest. I liked that. We would all go out and dad showed me how to pick mushrooms, and we laughed."

"We don't pick mushrooms in America. Picking mushrooms is evil. In America we go to the store and buy mushrooms. That is why we left Russia, to buy mushrooms."

"Yes, I remember, you bitched the whole time about picking the mushrooms."

"You're an ungrateful little bastard, you know. You, Sasha, and even Lizaveta!"

I look at her with rage and say, "Listen right now. Don't you ever speak Lizaveta's name again."

She looks at me in silence, knowing I mean it.

I say, "I know how you treated Lizaveta, I saw it. I know you like to tell people that Lizaveta was schizophrenic and all kinds of other shit, but I know. I'll die knowing."

She sits in silence.

I go outside and put the letters in my car and walk over to my father. He's feeding his rabbits. My father always has rabbits.

"Hello."

He looks at me with no emotion and says, "Hello."

"How are the bunnies today?"

"Fine."

I realize talking to him is fruitless. He will always remain a person who lets his misery eat him. He knows, like many working men, that keeping one's misery does not kill a man; starvation and heart attacks do.

I leave. I don't even say goodbye.

It doesn't matter.

He doesn't care.

He has never expressed a hate for anything, not the Soviet Union or for America, but he hasn't expressed love for anything either. All he has ever really done is work and brood.

I look at him from the car and see a sad automaton taking care of his rabbits. His only real happiness in life, two little rabbits that he pets and feeds every day. He has never shared memories of his childhood with his children, never spoken of any political beliefs, never cried, never really shown emotion at all except for a generalized brooding over something which he will not speak about. But there he is, a man feeding and petting rabbits.

14.

I'm sitting here at Sweet Jenny's.

Chang is beside me drinking rum and Coke.

Life has really become pointless.

We are drinking on a Monday.

How sad is that?

I look at Chang and say, "Chang, I believe these are my last days."

Chang doesn't even respond.

"Chang, everything is getting on my nerves. Even this chair I'm sitting on, it's hurting my ass."

Chang doesn't look at me when he speaks. "You're right. We should die."

"I know."

"Are we immature? Is this what thirteen-year-old emo kids talk about?"

"Emo kids are asses."

"When is something good going to happen? Something good happens all the time to other people. Not to us. We are like in some no-man's land where everything is dead and stupid and not remotely satisfying."

"I gotta shit."

I get up and walk to the bathroom.

I feel demoralized walking to the bathroom.

I feel like I should lie on the floor and die.

I get into the bathroom and sit down to shit.

I put my head in my hands.

There is no hope.

There isn't even a newspaper to read in here.

And it stinks.

I let out a huge fart and plop a turd in the toilet.

The water splashes and hits my ass.

I hate when that happens.

I remove my hands from my face and look around the shitter.

There's something in the corner of the shitter.

I pick it up and look at it.

It's a pill bottle.

I open the bottle and look inside.

Holy fucking shit, it's a bottle of Oxies.

Somebody must have dropped it.

I quickly wipe my ass because if I know anything about drug addicts, they are going to come looking for their shit, and I have no urge to give up this bottle of Oxies.

I don't wash my hands. I hurry out of the bathroom and sit back down next to Chang.

I tap Chang's shoulder.

"Yeah."

I look around the room to see if anybody is looking and whisper to Chang, "I found a whole bottle of Oxies in the bathroom."

"Are you fucking serious?"

"Yeah, look."

I slip the bottle out of my pocket.

Chang looks at it and says, "Holy shit! Some drug addict is going to be pissed."

"Yeah, I know."

Chang looks serious and says, "We don't do Oxies. What are we going to do with them?"

"Sell them, dumbass."

"Oh, good idea. How much can we get?"

"There looks to be like eighty of them in here. That's fifteen dollars a pill. That equals twelve-hundred dollars."

"Money."

"Yeah, money."

"Who are we going to sell them to? We don't have any friends."

"To strippers. We know a bunch of strippers who love Oxies."

"You're right, we do."

"We are badass gangsters now."

"Yes, we are. Vasily and Chang, badass gangsters."

"I'm thinking we could take the money and take a little vacation. We could go out west and meet some of our MySpace friends. How's that sound?"

"Good."

"I'll be over around ten tomorrow and we'll start selling them, cool?"

"My life is so awesome."

A man with grey skin and acne throws open the door and rushes to the bathroom in a panic.

Chang and I laugh.

15.

Chang and I pull into the Tally Hotel parking lot.

Nadia lives in 408.

"Nadia is a stupid cunt," Chang says.

"I know, but we need to sell these pills and she'll buy them."

"Fine, let's go."

We go up the stairs to Nadia's room.

Knock.

The door opens after two minutes.

Nadia, a young attractive woman with grey skin and acne, motions with her hand for us to come in.

Chang and I go in and sit on the bed.

Nadia sits on the other bed. She's talking on the phone, saying, "Motherfucker, I don't need you. Who the fuck you think I am. I'm Nadia. What the fuck. Those guys are here with the shit. I need the shit more than you. Who the fuck, what the fuck, I'm Nadia. I know that ain't my real name. What the fuck? I gotta go. Go fuck yourself!"

She says, "Okay, I got a hundred dollars. Either you get the hundred dollars or do you want blowjobs?"

"I want a blowjob," Chang says.

I punch Chang in the arm and say, "Shut the fuck up, Chang. We're here for the money. Give us your fucking money."

Nadia says, "You don't like blowjobs? You gay, Vasily?"

"I ain't gay bitch, I want the fucking money."

"Vasily, you a badass now or something? Usually you sit around moping like a fuckhead."

"Listen here bitch, I've been badass my whole life."

Chang giggles.

"Shut the fuck up, Chang!"

Chang continues to giggle.

"You boys need blowjobs?"

"We don't need fucking blowjobs. We need money."

"I got money, but I want to keep it. I want to give blowjobs and keep my money."

"Where's the money?"

"Listen, for twenty of them, I'll do anything."

"Anything?"

"Yeah, anything," Nadia says.

"I'll give you one if you fart on Chang's face," I say.

"You want me to fart on Chang's face?"

Chang interrupts and says, "Shut the fuck up. I don't want her farting on my face."

"Chang, you told me you like that. Here's your chance, take it."

"All right, okay."

"Do we have a deal?" I say.

"You want me to fart on Chang's face for one free pill and I still give you the hundred dollars for seven pills. So I will get a total of eight if I fart on Chang's face?"

"Yes."

"Okay. Clothes off or on."

"Take the bottoms off. He needs the full blast," I say.

Nadia looks at Chang and says, "Lie down."

Chang lies down on the bed.

Nadia stands and takes off her black stretch pants.

She gets up on the bed and puts her ass over Chang's face.

Chang looks really happy. It is kind of disturbing because he barely ever smiles and now he looks like a ten-year-old on a roller coaster.

Nadia pushes and lets one blast, a big rumbling disgusting fart on Chang's face.

I laugh hysterically.

Nadia begins laughing.

Chang smiles.

Nadia sits down, but doesn't put her pants back on.

I'm kind of turned on but I want the money.

Chang lies on the bed, smiling.

Nadia says, "You boys are fucked up. But I kind of liked it. I think I'll start doing that with all my boyfriends."

"How many boyfriends you got?"

"Anyone that gives me free Oxies is my boyfriend."

Nadia gives us the money and we give her the Oxies and leave.

We're in the car.

Chang says to me, "You acted like a badass. It was silly."

"Dude, you gotta act like a badass. We're drug dealers. Drug dealers are badasses."

"I'm five-five and a hundred and thirty pounds."

"Don't be a pussy. Man up."

"I like when bitches fart."

"So do I."

"Where are we going?"

"To that strip joint in Warren."

16.

We are sitting in the strip joint.

It looks like a country western bar with a pole in the corner.

Everyone here is poor and fucked. A bunch of weathered guys sitting around waiting to die.

Nobody looks happy.

Some are laughing, but even their laughter doesn't really seem like happiness.

I say to Chang, "Look around for a dancer with grey skin and acne."

"What the fuck are we doing?"

"Making money."

"Is this how people make money?"

"This is how poor people make money fast."

"Oh, okay."

I spot a girl with grey skin and acne.

I don't know who she is.

I hit Chang on the knee and motion to the dancer.

Chang looks and says, "That's it, that's money."

"Yes, money."

The dancer goes up on the stage.

I go over to the stage and sit.

She comes over.

She's a thin white girl with a face that looks broken.

She bends over and shakes her ass.

She pops it.

She turns around and opens her garter for money.

I put a dollar in and say, "You need Oxies?"

She looks at me and without doubt says, "Yes."

"Come over when you're done."

"Okay."

I walk back to Chang.

I say, "She wants some, we're making money."

"Good, money."

"Yes, money."

The dancer gets off the stage and walks over.

Money!

She sits and says, "You got some? How much?"

"Fifteen a pill."

"Sounds good."

She hands me one-hundred-fifty dollars.

I hand her ten pills.

She doesn't look happy.

She walks away without saying thank you or goodbye.

"That was easy," Chang says.

"Yeah, it was."

"There are still eight more strip joints in the area. We're set."

"Yeah, I know. We've made it. We're real drug dealers."

Then a large black man sits down next to me and says, "Do you have a fucking problem?"

This is not good.

Think. What would a real drug dealer do?

"No," I say.

"I have a problem."

"What's your problem?"

"You."

This is really fucking horrible.

He says, "This is my turf. I sell Oxies here."

"Oh, I'm sorry."

"These are my bitches."

"I'm going to leave now."

"That is a good fucking idea, and if I see you selling Oxies in here again I'm going to beat your ass."

"Okay, I understand the situation."

I look at Chang and say, "We need to get the fuck out of here."

Chang looks at me with terror and says, "What happened to badass Vasily?"

"Shut up, Chang. Let's go."

We get the fuck out of the strip joint.

We are outside and Chang says, "Did we almost die?"

"No, ass-fucker. We're fine. There are only like three murders a year in Warren, and usually one of those is some crazy white woman who kills her husband. There is a difference between Youngstown and Warren."

"You're right. We did almost get our asses beat though."

"That's true."

We are in the car driving down the street.

I say, "This sucks."

"What sucks?"

"This drug dealing shit. We gotta drive around looking for people to buy drugs. Drug dealers usually have a house where they sell drugs. But nobody knows we have these Oxies, so it isn't like we can sit in our house and play video games and wait for people to come over to buy the drugs. Instead we're out driving around like dumbasses looking for Oxie-heads to buy this shit."

"I know, this is really lame."

"Being a drug dealer is really hard."

"You just told me this was easy money."

"It is. It isn't like we're sweating."

"Let's go find Kathy and get her to hook us up with a drug dealer to sell this shit to."

"Good idea. That would totally be better than dealing with these crazy bitches."

17.

We're at the Lampost Lounge again.

Life is awesome.

It is dark and not smoky because of the new smoking laws.

It is lame.

I want to sit in a dark and smoky bar, but I'm just in a dark bar instead.

"Chang!"

"What?"

"You know what is wrong with this country?"

"It seems fine to me. Everybody is miserable. I've never expected anything less of life."

"That's good, but I'm not talking about elevating misery. I'm fine with misery, I'm used to it, I've grown up miserable, and now I'm a miserable adult. That's fine, but I'm not talking about that. I'm talking about when our fucking government infringes on our right to be miserable. We should be allowed to smoke in bars and get cancer."

"That's true. We should be allowed to ruin our lives through free will."

"Yes, let us ruin our lives!"

"We're miserable no matter what. We get paid shit to work our asses off, gas prices rise every day, everybody is on anti-depressants or coke or Oxies, our daughters get pregnant at twelve, life is all-around miserable, and they care about smoking," Chang says.

"Yes, motherfuckers!"

Kathy finally finishes a dance for a customer. She comes over and says, "What do you boys need?"

Chang protects his crotch.

"We need to find a drug dealer to sell Oxies to," I say.

"Where the fuck did you assholes get Oxies?" Kathy says.

"Mind your own fucking business, and give us a name," I say, like a badass.

"So now you're a badass, Vasily?"

"What do you want?"

"Twenty dollars."

"Okay."

I pull twenty out and give it to her.

Kathy says, "All right, I'll make a call and tell the person you're coming over. I'll be right out."

Kathy walks to the dressing room.

Chang looks at me and says, "She's going to set us up and we're going to get shot."

"No, we aren't."

"What makes you so sure?"

"It isn't like we're going to go in there and piss them off. Drug dealers shoot people that piss them off. We're going to go in, get the money, hand over the pills, and leave. That's all. None of that could result in us getting shot in the face and dumped in the Mahoning."

"No, we're dead," Chang says.

"No, we are not, we're fine. Listen, we tell them our names, they will instantly recognize that I'm Russian and you're Chinese. They will assume that I'm related to people in the Russian Mafia and you're related to people in the Triad."

"That sounds insane. My dad owns a Chinese takeout place."

"Yeah, so, who gives a fuck. What else do we have to do besides pretend we are people we aren't."

"That's a good point. Being one's self all the time is taxing."

Kathy walks out of the bathroom, comes over and says to us, "Okay motherfuckers, the guy said you two can come. He's at 45 East Evergreen in Youngstown. It is a two-story green house off Market Street. You know where that is?"

"Yeah, who doesn't," I say.

"Either of you want a dance?"

"No thank you, we gotta go."

"See ya later, assholes," Kathy says.

Chang and I head out the door to Youngstown.

18.

Chang and I are driving down Market Street.

Chang says, "This place is a shithole."

"No shit."

"It looks like ruins."

"It is ruins."

We stop at a red light.

We watch an older white guy with messed-up hair and an unshaved face sit on a park bench. An older black guy stumbling a little walks over and sits next to him. The older white guy hands him something and they both sadly laugh.

"This is really bleak," I say.

"We need to sell these drugs and get on with our lives."

"These people live like this every day," I say.

"That's why I hide in my room on SSI. I'm hiding from this."

"You hide from everything."

"I know, I don't want to see the rich with their Hummers or the poor with their crack pipes or the blue collar laying concrete. I don't want it."

"Nobody seems happy about this," I say.

"No, nobody is. Since the Renaissance with the help of oil we have been building a nightmare. But we've been working so slowly building it, and each person does their own little thing, that we haven't noticed that we've built a nightmare, an absolute nightmare we don't want, we never wanted. We were five years old and didn't it want then, and we get older and we still don't want the damn thing. But we're trapped in it. We're all closed in by it. Either we obey the machinery of this monster, or the monster starves us, the monster exiles us to be alone, and who wants to be alone against the monster. The monster is too big, too enormous. It has too many arms, legs, eyes, and guns. The monster even has bibles and constitutions, the monster has laws with policemen and armies guarding the laws. It has television shows, book companies, radio stations, it has the food, the water, the electricity and the oil. It has everything, and it is not operated by humankind any longer. Back in the day one tribe could kill another tribe and take their shit, but there is no tribe. There is the monster, and even if one of the big businessmen decided one day to not be part of the monster, the other big businessmen would kill him, because there is no human behind this. This monster we call civilization, this giant we have built with our minds and hands is now beyond our control. We don't control the monster anymore, it controls us," Chang says.

"It terrifies us into submission by being so huge."

"It encompasses everything. There is nothing the monster

has left untouched. We eat the monster's food, we drink the monster's water, we watch the monster's television, and all at the same time we are the monster. The monster has a place for everyone, if it be homelessness or the owner of a Subway."

I drive in silence.

I feel incredibly hopeless.

I start to wish that the drug dealers will kill us as soon as we walk in.

We are on the street.

The street has mostly abandoned buildings.

Several weeks ago, four men were shot to death in their living room on this street.

It looks like a good place for a horror movie.

We are at the house.

We walk in.

A large black man named Rick sits on a couch playing video games.

A fat white guy plays video games with him.

A white girl who seems to be talking to herself is sitting in the kitchen playing with scraps of paper.

And a skinny little black dude with acne scars is passed out on a loveseat.

We sit on milk crates in the living room.

Rick says, "You know Kathy?"

I say, "Yeah, I've known her from the Lampost Lounge for years."

"You know that bitch is crazy, right?"

He doesn't stop playing video games the whole time he is talking.

"Yeah, she doesn't seem right," I say.

"What your boys' names?"

"I'm Vasily and this is Chang."

"Vasily and Chang, those are some fucked-up names. What nationalities are you?"

"I'm Russian. Came oven when I was six."

"I'm Chinese. Came over when I was five."

"A couple of fucking communists. My dad fought the communists in Vietnam."

This shit happens to us all the time.

"Yeah," I say.

"Yeah, he said commies fight like hell. Don't fuck with them. So I ain't gonna fuck with you two. You both look kind of nuts to me."

The fat white guy looks at us and says, "You two do look nuts," and then he laughs hysterically.

Chang and I sit there knowing that we do look kind of nuts.

Rick says, "How many Oxies you got?"

"Sixty-two."

"Sixty-two Oxies. How the fuck did you two end up with sixty-two Oxies?"

"We stole them," Chang says with a tough badass voice.

"Nah, you two are part of the Russian Mafia or the Triad, aren't you?"

"We might be," I say.

"That's what I thought. I really shouldn't piss you two off now. Especially since I love Asian spas so much."

The fat white man laughs again.

I want to kill the fat white man, but I don't have a gun.

His drunken laughter and stupid-looking cornflower-blue jumpsuit pisses me off.

Rick says, "I'll give you eight-hundred. I need to make a profit."

I look at Chang. Chang nods okay.

We look at him playing video games and I say, "That's cool."

"All right."

Rick gets up and goes to the bedroom.

He comes out with eight one-hundred dollar bills and hands them to us.

We hand him the pills and leave.

Chang and I are driving home after a hard day of drug dealing.

Chang says, "We only have nine-hundred dollars. Is that enough?"

"Well, I get paid tomorrow. That will be twelve-hundred. Do you have any money?"

"I got two-hundred."

"Well, that's fourteen-hundred. That's a good amount."

"What if something goes wrong?"

"Then we call our families to send us train money home."

"Cool," Chang says.

19.

I'm in bed.

Can't sleep.

I can never sleep.

I sleep like five hours a day.

Thoughts keep racing.

Can't relax.

It is too painful.

The weight feels like a thousand pounds are sitting on my body.

My chest aches.

I think I'm a failure.

I don't know why.

Everything seems harsh and cruel around me.

People always seem to be getting worse.

Nobody ever seems happy.

There are no smiling faces in my world.

Sometimes something funny is said.

But no one walks around smiling.

No one ever seems like they truly care about anything.

No one seems like they matter to themselves.

They are driven by this desire to protect themselves.

To always remain unhappy.

Why does protection lead to unhappiness?

Who is trying to kill them that they need to protect themselves.

Why are they so afraid?

What are they so afraid of?

No one is going to stick them in prison for not owning a cellphone.

But they think someone will.

They act like a black SUV is going to pull up and men with huge machine guns will jump out and shoot them unless they own cellphones and respect the American Dream.

I'm fed up with this kind of behavior.

This environment is not conducive to happiness.

Everyone running around, stressing themselves out to be normal.

I don't feel normal.

I don't see how they do.

It confuses me, all this normalcy.

All this acceptance.

It seems like there should be more suicides.

Like there should be riots or small guerrilla wars.

But there's nothing.

This country is against me and my kind.

They have chosen against freedom.

Humans really enjoy digital graphics and sexy people and athletes telling them what to do.

That is why I can't sleep.

To be surrounded, engulfed, consumed by a world, having to operate in a world that depends on the marketing of steak and pork chops so I can wash dishes.

There are other things.

My mother never loved me and my father never speaks.

I grew up in a country thousands of miles away and I will probably never see it again.

I'm infatuated with a girl named Gina who won't date me because I don't attend a school of higher education and can't afford Nikes.

Outnumbered.

Tomorrow will be my last day of work and then I'm heading out west.

There will be something out west that doesn't suck.

Probably not.

I will find more hell.

But the hell will be prettier at least.

At least when I walk away from the commercial-loving assholes, I will be looking at a beautiful mountain instead of these damn abandoned steel mills.

20.

I'm sitting outside work on a milk crate.

I don't start for ten minutes.

The sky is a nice blue color and it is warm with a cool breeze.

I look at the building.

I look around the mall parking lot.

It all seems so horrible.

I'm just a man sitting here smoking a cigarette.

My life is meaningless as I sit here.

Jeremy walks up and says, "What are you doing?"

"Standing here, waiting to die."

"Dude, that is awesome. Can I ask you something?"

"What?"

I personally don't like to be asked questions.

"Do you believe in God?"

People ask me this all the time.

I find the question annoying.

"No," I say.

"I didn't think so."

I look at him and say, "You believe?"

"Yeah, of course."

"Jeremy?"

"What?"

"If you actually believed in God, you wouldn't need a second opinion. Believing in God isn't like cancer treatment."

"What?"

"Not too long ago, everyone believed in God, and no one asked that question. Everyone just believed. Now everyone asks that question. What do you think is next?"

"I don't know."

"No one even thinking about God."

"Dude, I don't know about you, but like, I believe in God, because if I don't, I feel really scared."

"I do believe that."

I'm standing in the office getting my paycheck.

Beth comes in and asks the manager, "Can I use the phone to call my baby?"

Her baby is like four.

Beth sits down and dials the number.

Someone answers, and Beth says, "Put Judy on."

Judy is her daughter.

Beth says, "Hey baby, did you ride your bike today? Oh you did? That's good. I love you too, honey. I just wanted to make sure you're having fun and you got to go outside and play."

I listen to her talk to her daughter.

It reminds me that my mother never called me and asked me questions like that.

Then it makes me hate the world.

Then to hate Judy.

But then I feel happy for a second.

At least someone is nice to their kid.

Beth seems like a good mom.

I'm not sure what that means.

But calling your daughter and telling her you love her is nice.

The world doesn't seem so dark for a few minutes.

I'm sitting outside smoking on a milk crate with Chris, the lousy dumb bartender, and Linda, the lesbian hostess.

Chris is your average man to the extreme. He looks average, he smells average, everything he does is average. Never more, never less.

Linda is cute with strong muscles. She smokes a lot of weed and complains a lot. She likes to tell me how she has gotten in physical altercations with her girlfriends.

Chris says, "Women are fucked up. They don't think straight. They're too emotional. It blocks out their judgment."

Linda says, "You're totally right. They do, they're all fucked."

I sit in silence. I'm surprised Linda would agree. It astounds me into silence.

Chris says, "They don't think like men. They aren't logical."

Linda says, "No, we aren't. You're totally right."

I can't stand these conversations.

Chris says, "They deceive you. Women fucking deceive you

into thinking things that aren't true. Then they give you the stab to the heart."

Linda says, "That's true. Women are liars."

I finally have to interject and say, "Men deceive too."

Chris says, "No, it's different. Men still think with logic."

I say, "Deceiving is our world. Our world is full of deception. We learn it when we are little, we learn it at work, we learn it at school."

They ignore me and keep talking.

I was interrupting their lies.

I walk back to the dish-tank and wash dishes.

I realize it now.

Fuck, this is horrible.

This deception.

This is all deception.

I'm standing here *pretending* I'm a dishwasher.

I'm deceiving the manager into believing I'm a dishwasher.

And I'm deceiving myself make-believing I'm a dishwasher.

The cooks are over there playing at being cooks.

They aren't cooks. They are only playing at being cooks.

None of us care about this steakhouse.

I have no interest in the dishes I wash and they have no interest in the food they make.

And this is how it is all over the modern world.

People build bridges they have no interest in.

People work at plants making little plastic parts they have no interest in.

People work in offices reading spreadsheets they have no interest in.

It is all pretend.

We show up to work and try to deceive the managers we want to be there.

And they reward us for being good deceivers with raises.

The owners deceive us by giving us money and convincing us we should *care* about the product they want produced.

And we deceive the owners by *pretending* we care about their product.

And the owners deceive the stockholders make-believing that they actually care about owning a chain of steakhouses.

Everyone deceiving everyone else for money to buy food and shelter.

And there's advertising, which deceives us into thinking that we need a certain brand of soap, a certain brand of cellphone, a certain brand of shoe, a certain brand of car, etc.

A massive game of deception!

And it is all transparent, right out there in the open.

These lies are so simple to detect we can't even see them.

They aren't lies like, lying about where you were last night, or how much you make, or that you weren't at a certain location when a murder took place.

These lies are right there, out in the open.

But we can't see them.

Because our parents were made of these lies.

And being our parents, they ingrained these lies in us.

And these lies make us.

We are these lies.

These lies engulf us to such an extent that our very identities are made, structured of these lies.

And then it hits me.

This mass deception we carry out every day has leaked into our romantic relationships.

And we learn when we are little that only through deception can we get the things we want.

It isn't work. It's deception.

Games must be played.

No wonder we can't see it.

We are it.

Fuck!

Shit!

This is terrifying.

That means that the modern world is like a dream.

That everyone floats around living in a dreamland full of lies and deception.

No, it's not a dream.

It's a fucking nightmare.

And I just woke up.

Tony, a cook who is always stoned, says to me, "They fired Larry."

"For what," I say.

"He stole shrimp."

"How much did he steal?"

"I guess the fucker took a whole box."

"That poor bastard."

"Dude, he was useless."

"No, he wasn't that bad."

"Dude, come on. He always fucked up your dish-tank and left a goddamn mess for us to clean up. Remember that night he got black shit all over the floor and left without cleaning it? And you had to stay to clean it after everyone left."

"Yeah, but he wasn't that bad."

"He got back on the pipe," Tony says.

"I figured that. He told me his mom kicked him out because he didn't have any money."

"That motherfucker wasn't kicked out. He went to some dude's house and they live there smoking crack together."

Then it pops into my head. This is my last day. "Well, that's the life of a crackhead," I say.

"They always get back on the pipe."

"They sure do."

It isn't very busy.

There are no dishes to wash.

I stand here looking around the kitchen.

The cooks are making food.

A hostess is standing by the soda fountain drinking from a paper cup.

The manager is standing by the window checking the food.

I'm doing nothing.

Time is passing.

The objects come into focus.

There is a lot of metal in the kitchen.

I wonder where all this metal comes from.

The kitchen smells like garbage and cooked beef.

No one is saying anything.

There isn't silence though.

The dishwasher makes noise.

The hoods above the grill make noise.

The fryers make noise.

I want to go home and lie down.

Life would be better right now if I was lying down.

Instead, I'm standing in the kitchen at work.

A kitchen.

What the fuck?

At the end of the night, Gina is standing on the back-line.

There is no one else back there.

She is filling her salt and pepper shakers.

I need to confess my love for her.

This is really dramatic.

I get some salad plates and carry them to the cooler on the back-line.

Gina is standing four feet from me.

I bring the salad plates into the cooler and drop them off.

Walk back out.

Gina is standing there.

I lean against a metal table and say, "Gina."

Gina doesn't look up and says, "Vasily?"

"Hmm, I want to tell you something."

"Yeah, go ahead."

"I'm going out west tomorrow."

"Oh yeah, that sounds nice."

"Yeah, and I'm quitting. And I wanted to tell you something."

She looks nervous.

"I wanted to tell you I have a crush on you, that I've had a crush on you since the first time I met you."

Gina stands there for a minute and says, "I know."

"You know?"

"Yes."

"How did you know?"

"You always do things for me and compliment me all the time."

"Is that okay?"

"Yeah. I gotta go finish my work though."

I look down at my shoes and Gina walks away.

BOOK 2

1.

Chang and I are in Indiana in the Jetta.

The sun is out and the sky is blue.

An all-around nice day.

It is good to travel down a highway on a pretty day.

Chang and I have never been out west before.

We don't know what we're doing.

We don't know if this is a good or bad or medium-okay choice.

We left Youngstown, that's what matters.

Our lives up to this point have been pretty much spent in the east.

Both of us have been to New York City and to Disney World.

Which is lame.

We are lame.

Since the car has no radio, Chang brought a small boombox to play CDs.

We are listening to a lot of classic rock like The Rolling Stones and Jimi Hendrix and also emo music like Sunny Day Real Estate and The Get Up Kids.

We know where we are stopping tonight.

In Illinois, there's a guy in his twenties with a blog called Iraq Jimmy.

On his blog he describes his miserable life in Iraq.

A lot of people check out his blog.

It gets over a thousand hits a day.

Chang emailed him and asked if we could visit and he said okay.

Chang and I are becoming less nervous as we get farther away from Youngstown.

Between the nice day and going somewhere far away, we feel better.

We are driving along and I say, "I'm glad we left."

"Yes, a good idea."

"It felt like my brain was being attacked by a giant squid."

"Our lives were ruined there."

"I would stand in front of Gina. And she would be there. And I couldn't speak. I would go home and listen to emo music and wait to die."

"I sat in my room. Time went on and on and on. I didn't know what to do. I still don't know what to do. I've never known what to do with myself. My parents never told me what to do."

"My parents didn't either. They didn't beat me enough," I say.

"I couldn't leave my house. I would go outside and the choice between walking to the store and walking to the park was too much. I thought if I was poor, like only living off the SSI checks I wouldn't have much to choose. At first I felt fine. I was on good medication, but then time passed and it all came flooding in again. Instead of being indecisive about what job to have, what woman to hit on and be rejected by, where I should drive my car, if I should go to the mall in Niles or the one in Boardman, I started worrying about little things, like what to eat, a sandwich or cereal."

"In the middle of the night I would tell Sasha I was going to the Waffle House and not go at all. I would go to the twenty-four-hour supermarket and buy flowers and drive out to Lizaveta's grave and put the flowers down and sit there. I would become scared though. I don't know why. The cemetery is a scary place at night. It is hard to live with her body lying immobile so close by. I always know where Lizaveta is. She's dead on Warren-Sharon Road. And then I would feel funny. I would feel like I was neglecting her dead body if I didn't go and visit her in the middle of the night. But what was there to visit? She is dead, that is her. That is Lizaveta, dead."

"She is dead."

"This thing bothers me though. Tell me if it bothers you. Sometimes you are listening to a person bitch and you know and have figured out that it is their fault. That no one caused it but themselves. But you can't say it out loud. You can't just say the truth. Because they are your friend and you like them, or they might not be your friend and you don't know them like that. So you sit there in some disgusting passive silence, withering away. And instead of actually saying anything, you say nice little things to reinforce their lies."

"Been there."

"Some nights I would drive around Youngstown and not know what to do. I would keep driving, staring at the same trees and houses. They all became like a monster engulfing me. But I had become so used to this monster I started to enjoy it. It was like I enjoyed suffering. What a horrible concept, the enjoyment of one's own misery. Maybe in some strange way I started to enjoy others' misery. I started listening to people talk for hours in bars and diners and at work on smoke breaks about their miserable lives. I wouldn't offer any advice or have any real interest in it. I just wanted to hear it. I think I wanted to eat their suffering. I loved my own suffering and I loved theirs. It didn't make me feel better about myself. It was like an addiction."

"No, I get you. I would sit in my room and listen to miserable music and let the misery overtake me. I would get myself all emotional. All crazy inside. All raving and mad over nothing. I couldn't even think of something to be miserable about. I would be emotional. I wanted to be emotional. I wanted to feel pain and hurt. Like in some way I was doing a penance. I started to think I deserved misery. That I deserved to be alone. To hate myself. But some days I couldn't think of any good sins. So I would let the music wrap me up in a little ball of tender emotion and force myself to hate myself," Chang says.

"People do not like happiness. It is like an enemy to them. Perhaps it isn't an enemy. Perhaps we've never felt it really. We've felt escape. I've gone to amusement parks and had fun, I've gone camping and had fun, I've had sex and had fun. But fun is not the same as happiness. I'm not sure what happiness is. Is it an emotion? Is it a way of life? Is it owning certain objects or having certain amounts of power?"

"I don't know happiness. Sounds like a word made up by someone very lonely."

"Probably."

I'm driving and Chang is looking out the window at Indiana's empty fields.

I say to Chang, "I remember when I was fourteen. I was at that skating rink in Cortland. It was a Saturday night. Remember how they would lock the doors and the kids could hang out there all night?"

"Yeah, I did that a couple of times."

"Yeah, it was one of those nights. I was flirting with some girl named Renee. She was so sweet and beautiful. She had bleach-blonde hair and soft milky skin. She had these green eyes that were so beautiful. I was so happy to be flirting with her. And we were talking and talking as we skated around the rink. And like two young horny fucks we started sitting next to each other. And eventually she let me kiss her cheek. It was nice. Then we kissed on the lips and that was great. I think about that sometimes when I can't sleep."

Chang says, "I was fifteen and at a party. It was a huge party. Like kids from three schools were there. There were so many people it was fucking terrifying. Well, there was this girl named Dedra. She was a little plump. Personally I've always liked them a little plump. I like meat. Most men don't like meat. Actually I think most men do like meat. But they are afraid to admit it. To go on, Dedra had these big tits that stuck out firm and lovely. We went off into the woods. I wanted to get away from all the people anyway. They were starting to get on my nerves. And Dedra lay down in the woods and I got on top of her and I jammed my tongue deep in her throat. And I was so hard. I remember being so hard. I mean, I was fucking hard. I could have hammered a nail and killed an elephant with my cock that night I was so hard. But we didn't do it. We just made out."

"My parents sent me to a counselor. The guy was a total jackoff. He didn't understand me at all and had no interest in understanding me. He believed in God and at the same time reincarnation and Buddha and Krishna and all kinds of mystic crap. The guy was a total *lie-to-yourself machine.* The man had a lie for everything. I told him how I hated my mother and that she was a piece of shit. And he would tell me to understand where she was coming from. I fucking knew where she was coming from, from some shithole in Russia. I know what makes her crazy and narcissistic. But I have to deal with my mother on a personal basis. Her personality makes me hate her. Her personality makes me want to scream and run away. I can have empathy for her. But that doesn't mean I have to like her as a person," I say.

"That guy sounds crazy. Counselors told me shit like that too. They always told me there was a God and he was watching and that if I only let Him in my asshole then I would shit properly."

"One day, my guidance counselor told me that his dead son had been reincarnated as a rock, and that he sat down on his son one day and knew it."

"What the fuck does that even mean?"

"I don't know. That he is alone and is making shit up in his head to feel better about being trapped in a world where people die and nothing makes sense," I say.

"I think if I believed in an afterlife, I would have become a Buddhist monk. I could have done that, sat all day and done nothing. I would have been silent. I would have sat, not spoken and alienated the other monks."

"Sometimes I think that about myself too. I think I would have become a Franciscan friar. I could have done that. Went around being nice and reading the Good Book and everyone would have kissed my ass trying to get to heaven."

"Yes, too bad we are fucked and don't believe in anything."

"We don't, do we?"

"We believe that we can't walk through walls," Chang says.

"Yeah, and that taking television news as truth is a mistake."

"Yeah, we believe in all kinds of things. We believe in the healing power of ice cream."

"And having too many friends is a bad idea," I say.

"Yeah, we are full of beliefs. We aren't nihilists just because we don't believe in God."

"No, we are totally moral. Godless and moral in a 1990 Jetta."

"Yes, life is good."

2.

We are in Nowhere, Illinois.

It reminds me of Youngstown but with more fields.

We pull into a shitty gravel driveway.

A small ranch house sits looking aged.

"This is Jimmy's house?" Chang says.

"This is where Mapquest brought us."

We go to the door.

I knock.

Chang and I are worried.

We've never met Jimmy before.

What if he tries to kill us?

What if he points a gun at our faces and ties us up.

Then rapes us for like twenty years.

Then we are found.

Then we will be in *Time Magazine*.

That would be horrible.

Having my picture on cable news.

A bunch of fucked Americans staring at my picture thinking about me being raped by Jimmy.

Then I realize I'm not rich and only when rich people get raped or kidnapped does cable news make a big deal out of it.

The door opens.

A large black woman stands in front of us.

She stands there looking at us like we are space aliens and says, "You here to see Jimmy?"

"Yes," I say.

She motions for us to come in.

She seems tired, weary of life.

The house is normal-looking.

There are pictures of family, grandparents, kids, etc.

The furniture looks almost new and the place is very clean.

Just a house where people live.

We all sit at the kitchen table and the lady gets us some water and sits down and says, "I'm Jimmy's mom. You can call me Tanisha."

We shake hands with her and tell her our names.

Tanisha says, "Jimmy's been having a rough time. He lives in the basement in a bedroom. He just sits down there. I don't know what to do. I want to get him some help, but he won't leave the house. And psychologists don't make house calls. So I'm stuck with him. I feel so uncomfortable knowing he's down there being nuts all day. I'm serious. He's fucking nuts. Something happened to him over there."

I say, "Does he often get visitors?"

"When he first got back, his old friends came over and tried to get him to go drinking and looking for girls. But he didn't want to. He kept yelling at his friends, saying one crazy thing after another. And eventually they didn't come over anymore. So now he writes on his blog and sits down there rotting like he's already dead."

Tanisha seems really sad.

Tanisha goes on: "I remember when he first joined the Marines. He left in the afternoon. His recruiter came to get him. And I was standing there looking at his young nineteen-year-old face. I remember being happy for him. It never occurred to me he would have to go to war. I thought he would go and see the world a little bit, maybe meet a wife somewhere, and learn some discipline. The boy was never good at making his bed and cleaning his room. I thought the Marines would fix that right up. Fuck, is all I got to say. Fuck."

Tanisha pauses, takes a drink of water and says, "I guess, I'll bring you down there now."

We follow her down the stairs into an old basement. In the corner of the basement is the door that leads to Jimmy's room.

Tanisha knocks and says, "Jimmy, you have visitors."

Over thirty seconds pass and Jimmy yells, "Tell them to fucking come in."

Tanisha looks at us like she is scared for us and turns back around and opens the door.

Tanisha doesn't go in.

So we walk into the room.

We sit down in plastic lawn chairs.

We look at Jimmy.

He lies on his bed.

A strong young man.

He is kind of pretty in a way.

His eyes, though, are hard and intense.

He scans us with his eyes like he is trying to figure out if we are going to try to kill him or not.

After he realizes that we are not there to kill him, he looks away and doesn't look us in the eyes again.

He stares at either his feet or the wall, but it is obvious he isn't looking at what his eyes are seeing.

The world around him doesn't seem important at all.

There is silence for at least two minutes before Chang breaks it. "How are you?"

Without deterring his hard gaze, Jimmy says, "My whole life has led to this moment."

Chang and I do not know how to respond to that.

Jimmy continues, "Here I am. I'm in Illinois. I was over there. Now I am here. There was sand. So much sand and confusion, confusion and sand. I was shot. That's why they sent me home. I was actually shot fifteen times in my bulletproof vest. But I got shot in my arm, and they sent me home. Shot fifteen times in my bulletproof vest. Each time I thought I was going to die.

"Confusion, confusion and sand, heat, unbearable heat. Road bombs, I was so confused. So paranoid, so scared, sweating, scared, paranoid. Alone. Each moment paranoid, each moment overcame me, each moment with its new thing to be paranoid about. I had never been so scared. No one knew. No sounds of fear came from me. I stood strong. The strong do not show their emotions. They shot me fifteen times and one eventually hit my arm. My arm, lay on ground, bleeding, wanting so bad to be somewhere else. Somewhere nice.

"I don't like being shot at. It is not a good time. But I woke up and got shot at. No one even told me why. There is a silence that pervades reasons. No reasoning. No one who considered reasons would have found themselves in such a paranoid moment, despair, confusion. I am not human anymore.

"Hate, endless hate is my life now. I hate even my own toes. I hate my toes. I look at my toes and hate them. I hate my toenails. I hate the bed. I hate my mother and the car she drives. I killed people. At first it was easy. Then it got harder. And harder. And harder. I have so many sins now.

"Sins are my life now. I have done things. Things that people shouldn't be told to do. I was told to do them and I did. I haven't slept for a long time. At night I sit in this room, during the day I sit in this room. I don't know what time it is. There are no clocks or windows. My mother comes with dinner. I eat some of it. Never all of it. I can't eat all of it. I keep living, allowing myself, to live. Each moment, looking at my shoes there, over there, somewhere, I wanted to be in a place that was nice.

"It isn't nice. It is here, in this room. Right now, I can't leave. There is no leaving.

"I thought I knew fear. You know, fear. I thought I knew it. I did not know fear. You don't know this. You two, you can't know this. I don't want you to know this. No one needs to know this. My mother told me the news about Cho, that kid who killed all those people. They stood there and let them-selves be shot. They were afraid. Terror struck them. They stood frozen. The bullets smashed into their bodies and they fell like beer cans shot by a pellet gun. That was ours, that was mine, every day, was that day, but I could not stand there in fear and let bullets tear me into death. I shot Cho. I turned and shot Cho, and I was Cho, and Cho was me. I was murder and murder was aimed at me. A million Chos, Chos every-where, Chos in this basement. We were told to enter a room of Chos as Chos to kill Chos to eradicate Chos while being Chos, and this was life, life as Cho, being Cho killing Cho, Cho trying to kill me, Cho shooting me in the arm. Cho is life. Cho is death. Cho is over there in the corner of the room. Cho out there staring me down behind the register. Cho at the assembly line. Cho folding boxes. Cho opening Christmas presents. I'm fucking Cho. Cho yells my name, calls me daddy. Cho like mites on my eyebrows. Cho comes out my nose onto a tissue. Cho driving car. Cho, I'm Cho. I am Cho. I am not Michael or Lebron, I am Cho.

"Everyone hates Cho. No one hates me. People say, you are a hero. I am not a hero. I am Cho. Cho is not a hero. Cho is Cho. Cho is murder rampage bullets death suicide. Crying tears. Fear. Cho was afraid. He was afraid of something. Cho entered afraid and he shot. I entered afraid and shot. Those who were shot were in fear. In fear they died. Like cinder blocks, all like cinder blocks, cold and solid, callous and hard, meaningless. Do you know meaninglessness. No, I did not here. Over there, I knew, I learned. The earth taught me. No God, earth. This earth is now my place. I am imprisoned here. This is my exile. No matter where I stand I am in exile. Exile is everywhere. Fear. They told me to do things. I did things. They paid me money. Not well. Cho did it for free. I did it for money. They did it for free also. I was paid. They blew themselves up for free and I shot them for money. Now, too much in exile to use grants. Now no fun. Here in this room, alone. A solitude I want. I can never be alone enough.

"I have one friend now.

"At all other times. With people. I am alone. In exile. No one can come to where I am. There are others like me. They were there with me. We cannot even reach each other anymore. There is no connection. We must live with our sins. A great injustice to the earth. We have taken. I am no longer human. The wind, leaves, sun, faces of people, no longer bring any happiness. Should have died fifteen times. Should be dead. Like Cho. Still alive. Still here. In exile. I renounce everything now. This room is my exile. I have placed myself here. Here is where I remain. There is no outside anymore, no happiness, anymore. I renounce everything. I place everything to the side and here I am. I am man. I must be. And because I am man I must exile myself. I must suffer for my sins. My face cannot be seen. They will know what I have done. And they will find me guilty. The word 'hero' only means guilty to me.

"Many men after war have post-traumatic stress disorder. That's what they say I have. They like to talk. I know what I have. I have loss of godness. A point comes, you kill so many people, and a power surges up in you. Making you like God. A man-god. Your fellow soldiers also become man-gods. A god surges up in you. And this god is unleashed many times. And if this man-god lives he will be unlucky. He will go home without gun and people to kill. And this man-god gets stripped of his godness. And then. Exile. The man-god sees he is no man-god. Then he succumbs to the fact that there was no man-god. A little girl came running toward us. She was so little. And somebody yells, 'She has a bomb.' In a split second I held up my gun and shot her face clean off. She lay there dead. A god among men. A hero. A god that takes life. A god that supplies wrath. A god that ruins.

"When I was little the story of Noah always fascinated me. The idea of a thing so powerful, a thing so strong, so unstoppable that it could will itself to kill all of humanity except for a few people. Can you imagine the will of God. Imagine that will. A will so strong, so sure of itself, so confident in its goodness, in its own morality, that it could kill ALL the humans except for a few. The Russians and Americans have had the power to do it for fifty years and have not had the moral strength to do it, but God did. That's the main story of the *Bible*, the thing that pulls it all together. The story that shows that God is stronger than all of us. Some think that God's kindness is unreachable by man. No, kindness is easy. But total destruction without remorse, that is what is truly awesome. Real power is a force that not only gives, refuses, but most importantly can take without remorse.

"As soon as that little girl hit the ground I knew the power of God. I knew what it meant to be God.

"Soon I took a bullet in the arm. They sent me home. And there I stood a god with no one to be a god over. The problem with making men into gods is that only gods can judge themselves. God answers to no one but God. Here I lay, answering to myself. In exile."

Jimmy falls silent.

Chang and I also remain silent.

There is nothing to say.

This man is beyond us.

We shake his hand and leave.

3.

We are sitting in a bar in Iowa.

A young girl named Charlene is the bartender.

The owner, her father, sits at the bar.

Chang and I have stopped to get a bite to eat and a beer.

We are eating in silence, happy about being alive, being in Iowa, when a man says to us, "How you guys doing?"

"Fine," I say.

"Where you from?"

"Ohio," I say.

"Fucking Ohio," he says, laughing.

"Where you from?" I say.

"Wisconsin," he says with pride.

"What are you doing out in Iowa?" I say. Chang says nothing.

"Working on the road. I'm with a construction crew. What are you doing out here?"

"Traveling through."

"Where you going?"

"Don't know. Down 80."

"You running from the law?"

"No."

"I'll buy you guys a shot."

Chang and I look at each other and I say, "Cool."

The man yells, "Three shots of Jack for us. I'm happy today."

He doesn't specify why he is happy.

Probably because he got hard for the first time in months and masturbated.

We all take down our shots of Jack.

The man goes, "You boys can't drink in Ohio I bet."

"We're from Youngstown. We can drink," I say.

"I doubt it."

I yell to the bartender, "Three shots of Jack."

Three shots get poured and we drink.

The man goes and takes a piss and I say to Chang, "We're gonna out-drink this motherfucker, all right. We're gonna show him what it means to be from Youngstown."

Chang nods a yes and says, "This motherfucker is going down."

The man comes back and yells to the bartender, "Three shots of Jack."

Charlene pours three shots.

We drink them down.

Then we drink more shots.

The man goes, "Is there a lot of niggers there?"

I say, "A lot of what?"

"Niggers. A lot of niggers? We got a lot of spics where I live. Not so many niggers," he says.

Then he goes on a tirade about unions, how unions are destroying America. And how abortion is evil.

The man goes to the bathroom.

"Chang, this guy is a fucking asshole," I say.

"He is a fucking madman."

Charlene thinks he's an idiot too.

The man comes out and says, "You two giving up yet?"

"No," Chang says, and I yell, "Three more shots of Jack."

Three more shots get poured.

Everything is blurry now and I'm crazy drunk.

But I can see the man struggle.

He doesn't look good.

He's wobbling.

He's dizzy.

He stumbles to the door and we can hear him vomiting in the parking lot.

We've won the drinking match.

I say to Chang, "I think we should kick his fucking face in for Jimmy."

Chang looks at me and says, "Yes, we should."

We go outside with fists clenched.

The man who owns the bar yells, "Yes, fuck that bastard up."

We're outside.

It's night.

The moon is beautiful tonight.

The man is on his knees, vomiting on the ground.

"Should we kick him while he's down," Chang says.

"Yes, without a doubt we should kick him while he's down."

Chang runs and kicks him in the cheek.

The man falls.

I kick him in the ribs repeatedly.

The man grabs his stomach.

Chang punches him in the face.

The man vomits all over himself.

I step on his nuts.

He grabs his nuts, vomit oozing out of his mouth.

His shirt is covered in vomit.

He lies on the ground, wriggling in pain, yelling obscenities about communists.

We laugh and I say, "Why don't you pick yourself up by your bootstraps, fuck-face."

Then Chang gives him a good kick to the head and the man starts to cry like a little bitch.

I look down at him and say, "That's Youngstown, mother-fucker."

Chang looks at me and says, "We need to get out of here."

We stroll to the car and take off down the highway drunk as fuck.

4.

I wake up in a tent at a campground a little ways into Nebraska.

Chang is sleeping.

He looks like a little mentally ill Asian baby.

I don't wake him up.

I go outside the tent and there it is.

Nebraska.

The campground is surrounded by cornfields.

There is no corn though.

You can see little bits of green popping out of the ground.

But it is too early in the season.

The fields are bare and stretch on for miles.

I have never seen the sky so big.

I've never seen so much while standing in one single spot.

It is beautiful.

The cornfields stretch out and encompass my view like looking at the ocean.

It is peaceful.

I sit on a picnic table and light a cigarette.

It feels good to be here.

I'm not sure where I am.

Somewhere in Nebraska.

It is nice to be in Nebraska.

The air smells good.

I don't recall ever getting a chance to smell fresh air.

In Youngstown, the air is not fresh.

If you leave a clean cup out to catch rain or snow, black soot is always left in the cup. Left over from the steel mills burning coal.

There probably isn't any black soot in the snow and rain here.

This is the prairie.

This is so cool.

Chang gets out of the tent.

He sits next to me and looks out at the prairie.

"Nebraska," he says.

I don't say anything.

We look at the Great Plains.

And let the breeze float over us like cool water.

It is early and the sun is shining.

Everything looks golden.

It makes me feel good inside.

"This isn't like Youngstown," I say.

"No," Chang says.

We sit for a long time there.

But eventually we get up, take showers in the community bathroom, and head down the highway.

5.

Chang is driving down I-80.

We have seen nothing but empty cornfields for the last three hours.

Chang's face looks happy.

I don't think I've ever seen the man look so happy.

He looks excited.

Chang stops at a lookout.

Which doesn't really look out at anything but huge empty cornfields.

There are little cement seats people can sit on.

We sit down and Chang says, "There's nothing. There's nothing *in the way*. For miles and miles nothing to see, nothing *in the way*. Open land and huge sky. I've been so trapped.

"So trapped.

"I've been strangled and pushed down, held down and everyone who ever got a chance grabbed me and tied me up. They wouldn't let me go.

"I woke up to stare at green trees and cars driving by, and the phone would ring.

"Everything always seemed so dead.

"It was dead but still coming down on me.

"Still pervading my being with structure, organization, and nonsense.

"I was down there in that little room, trapped, like a dog. Caged in. Then I came to Youngstown, and more cages. The cage of being different they put me in. The outsider cage. The weirdo cage.

"I suffered so much in that little hole at the bottom of that boat. We all suffered on that boat. But I was little, not an adult. My parents viewed it as life. But I had not been reared in misery yet. So I felt it. Then to Youngstown, then to another cage.

"I have suffered with the best of them.

"My suffering came from other people. They gave it to me, sometimes by force, sometimes I took it and made it my own.

"My family back in China were farmers. Now they sell General Tso's Chicken to Americans in Youngstown.

"How did we end up like this?

"How did we allow such a thing to happen?

"I became so scared and tired.

"But this land. This land, I'm okay here. I don't know if it is just the feeling of freedom I'm having being away from home or what. But I feel free here. Is feeling free such a bad thing? There is so much nothing. That is so nice to me. All this nothingness. A man like me could live here. I've been looking for this kind of nothingness all my life. This Nebraska. These Great Plains.

"That fight last night was fun.

"I would never have done that back home.

"But here, it seems natural to be having fun kicking somebody's ass.

"I don't feel *that* tension so much.

"Perhaps it'll come back. It always comes back.

"You know how they say people are the same everywhere you go.

"Well, Nebraska has less than two million people. Yes, they are the same, the same kinds of personality types exist everywhere. But there are a lot less here. A lot less motherfuckers to deal with here.

"I think I might stay here."

I start to think this is part of Chang's mental illness.

That he hasn't been taking his pills.

But his mental illness is who he is.

Chang might be nuts, but that's Chang. Chang is nuts.

"That's cool," I say. "I'll drop you at the next town."

"No, I go from here."

"From where? We can't even see a house from here. There are fields for miles. Do you have any money?"

"Give me a hundred dollars and I'll be fine."

"That's it? One-hundred dollars?"

"Yeah, I'm cool."

"Okay."

We get up and walk to the car together.

Chang fills a book bag full of random shit.

I hand him a hundred dollars.

The sun is bright and shining in both our eyes, making us squint.

Beads of sweat are going down our foreheads.

Chang looks at me and says, "You're a good dude."

He opens his arms and hugs me.

I hug him back.

It is a good hug.

A good strong hug.

We release our arms and I say to him, "You're a good dude too. Good luck."

He smiles.

He turns around and starts walking out into the endless cornfield.

I sit on a cement seat and watch him walk away.

He gets smaller and smaller as he walks.

The hugeness of the field engulfs him and slowly he recedes in the distance.

He is alone now.

But he is strong.

I cry a few tears.

I don't know if I'll ever see him again.

Chang is gone now.

Where will he go, what will he do?

Oh, it doesn't matter.

He'll be all right.

6.

The wind blows at the Rocky Mountains National Park.

I'm up high.

My ears keep popping.

Barely anyone is at the park.

The mountains are huge.

I'm smiling.

I'm really smiling.

I drive around the park, amazed.

Going crazy with love for this world.

I'm alone.

Chang is gone.

But I'm okay.

I drive around the park, aimlessly staring at the tall cliffs and bull elk that walk around peacefully in the pastures.

There is a light snow that covers the ground.

It is beautiful.

I can't believe that something so beautiful could be on the same planet with the shitty humans.

I find a place to camp.

I get out of the car.

A cold wind blows hard.

There is only one other group of campers.

A group of men spending the night in a Winnebago.

I view them as cheaters.

Real men sleep in tents.

I set the tent.

It is almost impossible with the wind blowing so hard.

The tent pegs won't stay.

It keeps pissing me off.

I look around and see mule deer walk slowly past.

They don't run like the deer back home.

Don't have a camera so I can't take pictures.

Have no camera or clock or cellphone. I'm free.

I stare at the mule deer for a while and continue trying to set up the tent.

I can't get the pegs in and the tent keeps getting tossed about by the wind.

I find large rocks and hold the tent down with them.

The tent kind of stays put, it will be good enough. When I get in it tonight, my weight will hold it down.

I get back in the car and drive around.

I don't know where I'm going.

Just driving.

It is all so beautiful.

It smells so good.

The wind so fresh.

Everything is so nice.

I'm amazed.

I'm happy.

I'm alive.

I'm actually happy to be alive.

This is such a strange and awkward feeling.

I don't feel tense or nervous or in a frenzy of emotion.

I don't know what to do with myself.

It is so unnatural.

I park the car and walk down a trail.

No one is around.

It's late May and barely anyone is at the park.

It is so nice.

I walk down a trail.

And eventually get to an open field.

Bull elk are standing around doing nothing.

I sit on a rock.

I can barely think, I'm so happy.

The bull elk do nothing.

They stand there.

They don't care about me, but I care about them.

I love them.

They are free out here.

This is their park.

I want to go up and pet them.

But they will probably kick me or bite me.

So I sit on a rock and watch them.

It starts to snow.

I head back to the car after an hour of doing nothing but watching bull elk.

I realize I'm hungry and drive out of the park.

There's a restaurant outside the park.

I go inside.

There are three people standing around talking.

They are wearing uniforms.

I'm the only person there.

A server leads me to a window seat and hands me a menu.

The menu has a bunch of expensive shit on it.

I order something cheap.

I stare out the window and watch the snow falling harder.

It looks like a blizzard.

But I know it isn't winter anymore and that the real Rocky Mountain blizzards have ended.

The server comes back and gives me my food.

I must look like a madman to her.

I'm unshaved, my hair a mess, I smell from sweating in Nebraska all day, and I'm wearing a ten-year-old camouflage hunter's coat.

I look pretty much homeless.

But I'm homeless in the Rocky Mountains.

I finish my food and drive back into the park.

I have to stop the car because some bighorn sheep are crossing the road.

Which is so cool.

I've never seen bighorn sheep.

They are so cool-looking.

They look like they could destroy my car with those horns.

Eventually the bighorn sheep cross the road and I get back to camp.

The tent is almost knocked over.

I fix it up and throw more rocks down and it's somewhat sturdy again.

It is night now.

The snow is falling hard.

Mule deer walk around the tent.

The middle-aged men with the Winnebago are sitting around a fire, drinking beer.

If I get attacked by a mountain lion, I can call on them for help.

I get into the tent and slip into my sleeping bag.

It is cold.

Almost freezing.

The snow is falling outside.

Wind smacking into the tent.

It is wild.

I feel really alive like this.

I don't know why.

It makes me happy.

All this nature.

All this life.

These animals walking around.

The giant mountains.

The huge sky.

It is crazy.

I've never experienced anything like this.

Being totally alone.

No one even knows I'm here.

I told Sasha that I was leaving but not where.

I didn't even tell Chang this is where I planned on going.

No one knows I'm here.

I'm a person without a name.

Without a home.

Without a past.

No one here cares who I am.

What class or what country I originated from.

What government I prefer.

The bull elk and bighorn sheep do not ask such questions.

They don't care.

The wind does not judge me and I have no reason to judge the wind.

Free at last.

At last, I need no escape.

I feel good now.

I'm cold but I feel okay.

Like not killing myself wasn't a bad idea after all.

Lying here in these mountains.

Makes me think if there are other things.

I'm missing.

Maybe I can live?

I don't know.

But I feel better.

Rejuvenated.

I have to pee before I fall completely asleep.

I go outside.

And unzip behind my tent.

A mountain lion walks out of the forest.

He walks no less than ten feet from me.

I don't move.

A fear rushes up in me.

But I attack the fear at once and calm my heart.

The mountain lion stops for a second and looks at me.

I can see its glowing eyes.

It is beautiful.

This enlarged version of the household cat that could kill me without much effort at all.

The mountain lion looks at me.

And goes on its way.

I finish peeing and go to sleep.

7.

I'm sitting at a lake in Northern California.

The trees are burnt all around me.

Everywhere I look is burnt trees.

Soon the fires will start again.

Soon summer will start and fires will blaze.

And more trees and more houses and more people will be burnt alive.

The lake is blue and beautiful.

If I had a boat I would go on it.

And sail around.

Maybe cast a line in the blueness.

But I'm sitting here.

Soon I will be at Jessica Benway's house.

Who is Jessica Benway?

An old lover.

An old friend.

She has a kid now.

She was married.

Jessica is no longer married.

She wrote me an email inviting me to stay with her.

I'm about two hours from her house.

I don't know if I want to go there.

It probably won't make me happy.

She doesn't seem very happy.

Why would I want to visit an unhappy friend.

But this is the trip, for better or worse.

This is the west.

Maybe I'll get laid.

Who knows?

8.

I'm in Jessica Benway's one room apartment, sitting on her bed.

She is in a reclining chair.

She has gained weight.

A good amount of weight.

The garbage can is full to the brim with empty Steel Reserve cans.

Cat Stevens's "Moonshadow" is playing on repeat on low in the background.

I look at my shoes and say, "So this is it?"

"Yes, this is it. This room. Those sheets. Those pictures on the wall. That sink over there, my feet and hands. This is my life now. This room is my life. This city and with me in it is my life."

"How did you get here?"

She rubs her right boob and continues. "I don't recall ever being a human. Ever really being alive. Ever having a chance. Ever knowing or not knowing what to do. I've always kind of floated along on a dream. There I was, once, a little girl, and the dreams picked me up and let me float on them. Not like dreams when you sleep or American dreams, or dreams of becoming a lawyer or doctor. Like a dream, a living dream I floated on. It was like a boat, or a car, a spaceship. I would cry sometimes, and I knew it was because the dream was not true. But I persisted. I held fast to the floating dream."

She goes to the refrigerator and gets a Steel Reserve. She offers me one and I take it.

We pop open our Steel Reserves and she goes on. "I'm dark inside. That's why you liked me. I reminded you of Lizaveta. I spoke to Lizaveta a couple of times and once, when we were alone, she told me in that thick Russian accent of hers, 'Jessica, all I ever wanted was freedom. I have always loved freedom. I wake every day looking for freedom. Where is this freedom Americans speak of? I look and look and find none. I find control and power, and the beaten and hurt, but no freedom.' Your sister is dead now. Her suicide was her freedom, Vasily. She felt controlled and dominated. She knew that life is a scam. She knew that her only purpose in life was to work and pay bills and the only virtue she needed for that was a self-loathing fortitude. But not a fortitude to win a war or fight oppression, the fortitude to show up to work on time for thirty years, do our job good enough to not get fired and eventually reach retirement to die alone with shit in our pants in a decrepit nursing home.

"Lizaveta killed herself as an act of freedom. As an act that said to the world, 'You think you have me, but you don't. I am still free and can do at least one thing you can't stop.' And Lizaveta did it. She died free."

Jessica takes a large drink of Steel Reserve and says, "Have you noticed I'm fat now?"

"You put on a little weight."

"No, I'm fat, Vasily. I'm fat and washed-up."

"You look fine," I say.

"No, I got fat on purpose. Listen. I wanted Charles to leave. He wouldn't leave. So I got fat. He told me that shit about not minding and all that shit humans say to make each other feel better, even though they feel horrible about the situation and what's going on. He wouldn't leave so I cheated on him. But I've gotten used to being lazy and drinking beer. And these stretch marks, do you wanna see my stretch marks?"

"That's okay, I believe you."

"No, I want you to see what that baby did."

Jessica stands up and pulls her shirt up and shows me her stretch marks. It looks like a truck ran over her belly.

"Do you see what that baby did?"

"Yeah."

"I'm in hell and I'm fat."

"You're being really dramatic."

"I'm being dramatic. My life is ruined. Oh, Jessica Benway's life is ruined, who the fuck cares. You don't care? You know why, because you can leave. You can leave any time you want. You don't have a kid and an ex-husband. You don't. You're Vasily and you've always been smarter than that. Well, fuck, Vasily, I'm not. I'm not smarter than that. I make mistakes."

"I'm a fucking dishwasher. Don't make me feel guilty."

Jessica stands up and starts pacing and using her arms to make points.

"Listen, Vasily, you must understand, I'm fat and washed-up. Who wants a fat woman with kids? No one does. I'm alone now. But you know what, I don't hate Charles. I don't. I think he's a nice guy. But I didn't want to live in the same house with him anymore. That's all. Our life was fine. We had money and a kid and cars and the bills were getting paid on time. We were living out here in the west and life was totally tip-top. But goddamn, I was bored. You know what I'm saying, Vasily?"

"Yeah, I got you."

Jessica sits down and says, "Did you think if you came here you would recapture something? Because it seems kind of melodramatic that you came here."

"I didn't come here. I came out west and you're here."

"Oh, make me feel unimportant. I thought we were going to have a moment. And you go and ruin it with facts."

Jessica and I lie down together on her bed to go to sleep.

I'm in my underwear and she's in a pair of pink pajamas with bunny rabbits on them.

Jessica says in the darkness, "I don't think we should have sex."

"Why?"

"Because I'm really sleepy and it wouldn't help my self-esteem."

"It wouldn't help my self-esteem either," I say.

"Vasily, you don't need self-esteem."

"Why don't I need self-esteem?"

"You're Russian."

"Huh."

"I have no idea what that means. It's an excuse. I can't have sex right now. I don't know what is wrong with my pussy. It is wide right now."

"Wide?"

"Yes, it takes more to fill it. You will be lost in there. You are average, but average won't cut it with this hole."

"You're saying you're embarassed because your pussy is big now."

"Yes, and I can't do it. My arms won't do it anymore. I'm afraid. I know what the cost will be."

"What will the cost be?"

"Listen, I know you. I know myself. I'm ruined. Do you want to have sex with a ruined woman?"

"I never mentioned having sex with you. You did."

"Then why are you grilling me with questions?"

"I'm just talking."

"This is hurting me. This whole thing."

Jessica gets up, opens a bag on the floor and takes out a pill bottle.

She opens the pill bottle and takes a couple of pills and stumbles back into bed.

"That was dramatic," I say.

"You don't know drama."

"I don't know drama?"

"I am like da Vinci when it comes to drama. You are like a monkey drawing with crayons."

"That was so weird."

"Remember that time I cried for forty minutes so you wouldn't go to the bar?"

"Yeah, I do."

"That was great, wasn't it? I just kept crying. It was wonderful. I could have stopped at any time, but I kept it up. Crying away until you gave in."

"I knew you were acting."

"I know you did, but you knew I wouldn't stop acting until you gave in. And I knew you giving in was just acting and that you really wanted to go, but I wanted to exert power."

"Remember that time you came in the living room and accused me of being a brat because I asked you politely to get me a glass of water."

"Yeah, you sucked that day."

"Why did I suck?"

"Because you didn't give in. You sat there. I started crying and everything. I even brought up things you did in the past that were mean. And you sat there like a fucking rock staring me down. It was horrible."

"So can I fuck you?"

"I don't know. All right, but don't touch me."

"How am I supposed to not touch you if we're fucking," I say.

"I'm going to roll over on my side. There's lube over there. Lube yourself up and put it in and you can pump for like ten minutes, okay?"

"That sounds cool."

I take my boxers off and get the bottle of lube.

Jessica pushes her pajama bottoms off but leaves her shirt on.

She rolls over on her side.

I get behind her and insert my penis.

I pump.

Jessica makes no noise.

She stares at the wall.

I ejaculate.

I pull out and go to sleep.

9.

Leaning against a giant redwood.

Alone.

Almost to the Oregon border.

I look up at these giant old trees.

They stand what seems like miles above me.

There are almost no people walking around.

Jessica can have her pills, I want these trees.

People pain me.

Instead of saving up and taking trips to the redwoods.

They purchase expensive cars, clothes, televisions, and houses with rooms they don't need.

They sniff coke and take pills and gamble in hot-ass Las Vegas.

I made it here across America with little more than a

thousand dollars and a car I bought for three-hundred dollars.

Hardly anyone is here.

No one cares about these trees.

I've never had any interest in seeing the Parthenon or the Coliseums of Rome, or the Vatican.

To me they are no different than the abandoned steel mills of Youngstown.

Old discarded objects built by man during times when a small group of people had money, and the majority made it for them.

And most of all, what ruins symbolize to me is that you will die one day.

These giant trees, taking hundreds or thousands of years to grow to their enormous height, had to kill no one, had to oppress no one, had to ruin nothing, to attain their height.

These giant redwoods don't signify death.

They tell me about the earth.

That I'm part of it.

10.

In the Oregon Cascades, I'm driving down back roads looking for Misail Poloznev's house.

I worked with Misail at a factory in Youngstown.

Misail had left it all.

He had grown up with money, had gotten a good education at a private college, and had good jobs working on computers.

He left it all.

He never spoke to his father and his mother was dead.

He cut his family ties.

He sent me a letter several months ago.

Dear Vasily,

I moved to the Cascades. Life is good here. I grow my own crops and fish in the stream. If you ever feel like visiting me you can. There are not many I want to visit me, so don't be handing out my address. I'm free now.

I do not have a phone, running water, or electricity. I do not even have gas. So be prepared, and bring some toilet paper.

My life is good now.

Use the address I wrote on the envelope to find me.

Your Friend,
Misail Poloznev

11.

On a back road about forty-five miles east of Eugene, I get to the point where Mapquest says Misail's house is.

There's a mailbox.

I read the numbers.

It is at the end of a driveway that seems to go off into the forest.

I drive down the driveway.

The driveway is overgrown, like no one has driven on it for a long time.

It is beautiful.

There are small redwoods and pine trees everywhere.

It smells good and the breeze is nice.

I pass an inexplicable cellphone tower in the forest.

Eventually, after five minutes, I arrive at what looks like a field with crops and a small octagon-shaped hut.

I pull up and park on the grass because there is no real place to park.

I get out and look around.

There doesn't seem to be anyone here.

I walk up to the hut and knock and no one comes to the door.

I yell, "Misail! Misail! Misail!"

Someone screams, "Who's here? I'll kill you!"

"It's me, Vasily!"

A man comes over the hill.

It's Misail.

He's naked.

Misail looks strong.

Veins stick out of his forearms.

Every time he moves a finger, a muscle is flexed in his arms.

As he gets closer I see his face.

It looks weathered.

His eyes don't seem to be looking at anything.

They seem dead.

Hard and cold.

He looks like he could reach out and rip the life out of me and not be concerned with it.

He looks like a devil.

What causes such a look on a man's face?

Is that what a man looks like when he throws his complete past away and decides to build his own future without regard for one law or tradition made in the last 3,000 years?

He comes over the hill and says, "Let me put some shorts on."

He walks by and waves for me to come into the hut.

The hut is a nice small place.

It has a fireplace, a twin bed, and the outer walls are bookshelves filled with books.

I look at the bookshelves and see books by Nietzsche, Sartre, Richard Wright, and also many books about gardening, survival in tough environments, and how ancient civilizations and tribes from Latin America to Africa lived.

Misail waves for me to follow him outside.

We walk into the forest.

It is quiet except for the sound of bugs and an owl.

Misail doesn't speak.

I follow behind him a few feet.

We used to talk a lot but now he says nothing.

He doesn't even ask me how my trip was.

We get to a small creek.

He grabs two fishing poles leaning against a tree.

He hands one to me without speaking, goes over to a box, opens it and puts a worm on a hook. He motions for me to do the same.

We sit together on the ground.

We cast our lines into the water.

Misail's silence continues.

I do not know what to say. He was always the one who spoke when we knew each other in Youngstown.

Misail sighs and says, "I don't have anything to say. I haven't had to deal with the shit of the world for a long time. There isn't anybody else here to bitch about. No one is here to make fun of, analyze, criticize, or make drama with. When I talk all I hear is silence. Sometimes rabbits eat my crops and I bitch about that in my head. Sometimes spiders get in my hut and I bitch about them in my head. But besides that, there is nothing to say. In our society, we grow up hearing and eventually talking about only a few things. We talk about ourselves and our problems which involve other people, but there are no other people here to give me shit. We talk about our ambitions and accomplishments, but there is nothing to accomplish here. The forest offers no degrees, raises, or awards. We talk shit about other people, but there are no other people here. We talk shit about ourselves, but we hate ourselves because we relate ourselves to others, and still there are no other people here. We talk about religion and government, but the redwoods have no religion and the rabbits don't hold elections. I'm sorry if I am not good company. But I must tell you this: I don't have any interest in hearing about why you're here. What people and their behavior, what political, sociological, philosophical madness has brought you here to me. I'm sure it is all true, that it is very important to you. But I'm sure telling me won't make a difference. Please sit here and catch a fish with me. If you would like to talk about the redwoods or about what types of fish swim in this creek, you may. I have heard and thought enough on the world of people."

"Okay," I say.

"Good."

We sit for a while and talk about the redwoods. Misail tells me the ages and what berries can be found in the Cascades and while we are walking back to his hut a deer walks by. We look at the deer.

I spend a week with Misail.

I help build a new bathroom.

Fish in the stream for a little bit.

Shoot the bow and arrow at a target.

Help take care of the garden.

Learn how to skin a rabbit.

The days are nice and I become rejuvenated a little.

It is a nice escape.

But it is too lonely.

Misail and I are sitting outside his hut.

The sun is shining and it is a beautiful day in the forest.

I say to Misail, "I have to go now. I've got to get back on the road."

"Where are you going to go?"

"The desert."

"What's in the desert?"

"I don't know, but it seems right to me."

"It'll be hot there."

"I don't mind. I can handle heat," I say.

"What are you gonna do for money?"

"Oh, fuck, who cares. Work somewhere I guess."

"Wait, hold on."

Misail goes into the hut then returns.

He hands me a wad of money.

I take it and say, "Thank you. You don't need it?"

"No, I have enough."

"Thank you, Misail. I'll be back one day to visit."

"If you never make it back, don't worry. I'll be fine."

"Okay."

I get my stuff from the hut and Misail and I walk to the car together.

I look at Misail.

He looks okay.

He looks like he made a choice he can live with.

I look at him and say, "What are you going to do?"

"Someday a bear will eat me and perhaps my life will come to some use."

I laugh, get in my car, and leave.

12.

I'm sitting on the hood of my car.

I'm in Nowhere, Utah in the middle of the night.

At a lookout that overlooks a valley where more dinosaur bones were found than any other place on earth.

At least that is what the little plaque says.

It is around a hundred degrees out.

I'm sweating on top of dry sweat.

Shirtless, wearing a bandanna to keep the sweat out of my eyes.

Misail gave me two-thousand dollars.

I don't know why he gave it to me.

I think I'll start over.

Maybe *be* someone new.

Who knows?

"It sure is hot out here," I say, laughing in the desert.

Two Old Lovers
Bring Their Guns

Around eleven o'clock at night the phone rings. It says on the caller ID Benway and a phone number. The name Benway and the phone number lead to my ex-girlfriend I had three years ago, Jessica Benway. I stare at the phone number and it all flashes in my mind, all seven years of weird hell I had with that girl. All the fights, all the yelling, and even some good times; there were good times. There had to be good times sometimes or I wouldn't have stayed. I remember the best times were when we weren't talking. Like watching television in silence or eating in silence or showering together in silence.

Sometimes I look at Benway's MySpace page. I stare at the photos of her face and think, 'She still looks kind of pretty. It is nice that pictures are silent.' Now I am not trying to say women shouldn't talk. I love to hear Isabella and Sasha talk. But Jessica was not my type. She was one of those classic leftovers from high school. We started dating in 10th grade, then we went out and broke up and went out again and broke up again for too long. Our problem, or at least my problem, was that if I totally broke up with her then I would have to admit high school was over and that I was totally an adult, and that was something I did not want to do and still today I don't want to admit such an atrocity.

But it's strange that she would be calling because from what her MySpace page says, she got married, had a baby and moved to northern California. Maybe she is home on vacation, I don't fucking know. This is terrifying. Picking up the phone is dangerous. Don't we already have closure? Isn't closure totally completed after you get married to someone else? Doesn't like Jesus come down and anoint the married couple in closure oil or something.

I pick up the phone.

"Hello."

"It's me, Jessica."

"Okay."

"I'm home on vacation and want to see you."

"Aren't you married and shit?"

"Yeah, so, I don't want to fuck you. I just want to sit and talk. My husband is back in California. I just want you to come over and drink coffee with me for an hour. That's all."

"There's a blizzard out there."

"I know you can drive well, don't fuck around."

"You are already hurting my feelings."

"Shut up. Just come over."

"Where? To your mother's house?"

"Yeah, to my mother's house."

"Are you going to kill me?"

"I'm not going to kill you."

"I think you might."

"No, no death."

"Okay, I'll drive over."

I hang up the phone. This is a bad idea. I know it is a bad idea. But fuck, it isn't like I have anything else to do. It isn't like Youngstown is offering a great night of fun besides getting drunk downtown, slipping on the ice on the way home, breaking my leg and freezing to death.

I go into the living room to talk to Chang about it. This is drama; I must soak up every minute of it.

Since I brought Chang home, he hasn't left. He has been sleeping on my couch not really doing anything for three days. The not doing anything doesn't seem to affect him; I have a computer with the internet so he is staying in tune with MySpace.

I walk in and sit on the floor. Chang is reading some used copy of the *Philokalia*, which is some deranged book written by solitary Eastern Orthodox monks who lived in the forest writing crazy shit five-hundred years ago.

"Chang."

He looks up from the book and says, "Yeah."

"I'm leaving to talk to Jessica."

"Your ex-girlfriend."

"Yeah."

"That sounds dramatic."

"I hope so, nothing dramatic has happened to me in a while."

"Didn't you say you impregnated Isabella."

"I'm not sure if I did. If she is actually pregnant that will be dramatic. But we won't know until and if she misses her period and then takes a pregnancy test. So currently I'm without drama."

"Bring back some bananas and some pop."

"Can I ask, why the hell are you reading that? You don't even believe in God."

"They're alone."

"Okay."

"Be careful, there is a winter storm warning."

I drive down roads covered in snow to get to Jessica's house. It takes forever. It is cold and the snow won't stop falling. Why would I drive through this snowy hell to see someone I haven't seen in three years, and for sure nothing will happen, and words will be said. There will be staring and memories brought up. But nothing will happen. It will result in nothing but me eventually leaving and picking up bananas and pop for Chang.

Oh yes, dumb drama will happen. Drama, the life force of Americans, like it is our religion now. When it became our religion I don't know. But it is now. God died and was replaced with drama. We all go to the altar of drama and pay tithes, we bow and pray at the altar of drama, of pseudo-emotions and play-acting. We love it. We love watching it on television, reading it, talking about it, starting it, ending it, being a side actor watching it, we love to hear about it, and the grosser and more despicable it is, the more we love it. The other day, a friend of some girl I know dropped his cellphone at a local sporting event and when whoever picked up the phone was looking for who owned it, they found pictures of naked eight-year-olds. My friend told everyone, we all listened intently, we all asked questions. She loved to tell us and we loved to listen. It was drama. It didn't have anything to do with us, but it was drama and we as good Americans considered it beautiful.

I get to her house and knock on her door.

This is a bad idea.

Jessica opens the door.

I look at her and she looks at me.

We are looking at each other, both thinking about the other one. I'm thinking about how she looks good. That I would like to touch her face and some other stupid shit. She probably is thinking about how she hates me and only brought me here to torture me for the sake of her self-esteem.

I go into her house. I know where everything is. It hasn't changed. Nothing changes at her house; it is like an inert rock on Mars.

I sit down at the kitchen table; she is still standing and says, "Do you want some coffee?"

"Yes please."

"You were always polite."

I sit there waiting for her to take out a gun and shoot me in the face. I close my eyes for a second, waiting for the end, but it doesn't come. So as to not seem so weird, I open my eyes and try to stay composed and functional. She is doing a much better job at staying composed and functional than me. She was always better at these things. She watches soap operas and Julia Roberts movies; she is a master of drama orchestration. She is a maestro and I'm a lame bassoon player when it comes to the art of drama.

Jessica sits down and hands me coffee. She is also drinking coffee. We are both drinking coffee, sitting across from each other, staring at each other, being dramatic.

"Vasily," she says.

"Yeah."

"How are you?"

"I'm doing fine."

"Our lives have gone on without each other."

"Yes, they have."

"Remember, how we said all those things. How we said we loved each other and would always be together, and we would get old and kiss each other's wrinkles."

I do remember it, but I don't want to admit it, but I say,

"Yes, we said shit like that several times."

"It wasn't true."

"I suppose it wasn't."

"People go on without each other. No matter how much feeling you have at one single moment, it fades. You scream and holler for this person, you tell everyone you meet about this single person you've met and are with, and how much you love them. But then it still fades."

"Are you talking about us or your current marriage?"

"No, he is like me. He watches the same shows, he likes bowling like me, he likes kids like me, we have common interests. It is true, our relationship has lost the passion of sex, but we have become like friends or partners in life. I'm not addicted to him, I'm just, well, friends with him."

"Would he say the same thing?"

"Who knows, I'm not going to ask. It doesn't matter. That is how it works." She drinks some coffee and lights a cigarette and goes on, "It is strange, there are loves in life, when you are crazy addicted to that person, you are crazy about them, you have crazy wild sex, you get into huge insane fights, like you can either do one of two things with that person: fuck their brains out or scream at them. That is what we had."

"That's probably because you resembled my mother and I resembled your father. We were living as children wanting our parents to love us. Not as who we actually are, and basing our relationship on logic."

"See, there it is. That's why I left you. You started talking about love like it is some goddamn science experiment. You refused to let yourself go anymore. And I guess from that comment you still won't. You used to fuck my brains out, and you used to fight with me all night. I loved fighting with you. As you say, I was getting to vent my anger at my father.

And I guess you would even say when you fucked me, I was getting the attention from my father I always wanted. But one day you stopped fighting. And you even stopped fucking. I went into the living room yelling my brains out at you and you just sat there. You sat there and stared at your shoes and waited till I stopped yelling. You used to fight and scream like a motherfucker. It was horrible to me. The game was over, the drama and passion had ceased to exist."

"I had grown out of my mother."

"And that made me a joke."

"No, it made you a remnant of a world I no longer wanted."

"So trash then, I was leftover trash."

"To say it bluntly, yes, trash. I truly did not hate you. You just seemed *in the way*."

"I don't understand. Did I do this to you? What the fuck happened? You just stopped one day, you stopped caring. Look at you now. You still haven't picked yourself up. You dropped out of school, and it has been three years and you still haven't returned."

"The meaning of my whole life was that I hated my mother but even though I hated her, I still wanted her to love me. That was my reason for being, that was the reason I was going to school was because I wanted her to be impressed by it. But two years passed and she never even looked at one of my report cards. I thought maybe if I dropped out she would take notice if I was doing badly, but she didn't notice that either. So I gave up trying to impress her, trying to get love, and by doing that, by saying goodbye to that part of my life, I said goodbye to you and to college, and perhaps to doing anything that would cause the slightest chance of impressing her."

"So you chose to never impress her again, and that means you can never do anything impressive ever again."

"No, I think it is like, since I cannot impress her, then what is the point of doing anything."

"Then your behaviors are still connected to her. You are still basing your daily activities off of her behavior," she says.

"Did you bring me here because you wanted to destroy me?"

"No, I brought you here because I wanted to tell you this. I want you to know and realize what you're doing. I keep tabs on you, I always ask about you when I'm talking to people who know you. It is just, I'm out west, I'm married, I have a kid, I'm doing okay. It isn't a great life, I'm nobody's hero, I'm not on television, I don't have a million dollars in the bank. But I'm sure as fuck doing better than you. You haven't moved forward since I've known you."

"No, I haven't. But why do you care?"

"I loved you for seven years. I woke every day for seven years and thought, 'I love Vasily.' That means a lot to me. If I didn't see you for twenty years and you died, I would still go to the funeral. We only have one life, as you always said, and before we die we look back on it, and I can't look back on mine without seeing you. I don't know if that makes sense, or is logical, but that is how I feel. And one day when my daughter gets older she will ask about my boyfriends before I met her father and I will have to mention you. I will speak the name Vasily to her. She will ask about Vasily and I will explain your strange ass to her."

Jessica pours us some more coffee and sits back down. We stop looking at each other. We stare at the table, at our shoes. But while we speak we don't notice them. Our minds are busy, our eyes are open, but in our minds we are trying to find what to say next.

Jessica says, "Vasily, why haven't you attacked me. I've been sitting here attacking you. But you say nothing. You used to be so good at arguing, you could tear holes right in me. You always broke through my wall of shit and blasted me with something I did not want to admit to myself. You were so good at analyzing other people, so apt at judging people's characters, of seeing past their lies. But now, you just sit there. Still sitting. It makes me think you don't care about me. Do you not think anymore? What is it?"

I don't like this conversation. Why doesn't she talk about when we went swimming at Willow Lake or something?

"Are you going to respond?" Jessica says.

"I realized that you wanted me to attack you. It fed your sense of masochism. The purpose of combat is to crush your opponent. To make them bend to your will. To make them fall to the floor, to give up, to show that they are weaker than you. I wanted to win the arguments, by attacking you; I was playing your game. The harder the blows I threw, the harder yours were. It allowed for too much chance. And also you wanted the fight, you wanted to yell. And if you wanted it, and you weren't getting paid for it, that means you somewhat enjoy it. So therefore even if you lost, there was a part of you that enjoyed losing. So my only chance was to reject the fight. To sit and stare, which made you frustrated and self-loathing. Which means I won the fight, I made you bend to my will. I could control my emotions, and by controlling my emotions I made you feel false, which killed you."

"I could no longer hurt your feelings."

"No. I suppose that meant I did not love you anymore."

"Can anyone hurt your feelings anymore?"

"Yeah, but after they do once, I'm done with them. They can go to hell for all I care."

"That sounds like a terrible way to live, not having any feelings."

"You mistake drama for feelings. Most of the feelings we have in this country are fabricated and mass-produced. Ninety-nine percent of them are false."

"You probably think the feeling I have for my daughter is false. You would probably assume revenge."

"You called it revenge, not me."

Jessica looks at me and says, "People need feelings. We need to tell ourselves things. What are we supposed to do? I've never had power, I've never done anything great, I don't even know how a person would go about doing something great. I'm an ordinary person and I have feelings, I like feelings, I like drama, it gives color to life. It makes it not so dense."

"Did I say anything against people having feelings? Did I sit here and crucify you for wanting drama. I came here, didn't I? That must mean I want drama. I want color in my life; I want life to have some meaning."

"But you reject so much of it. You fight yourself from having feeling. From letting yourself go. When we went to bars you just sat there and drank your beer quietly. You never went to parties, you never got drunk and started punching people like normal men do, you never went up on the stage at a karaoke and sang, you've never danced at a bar. When we went to punk concerts you wouldn't mosh. It is like you refuse to fully enjoy life, to just relax and flow with humanity."

"I can't."

"You know why? Don't be an asshole!"

I get the urge to grab her face and squeeze it but I don't and say, "I'm afraid."

"Well, why are you afraid?"

"People hurt each other. If I dance somebody will go, 'you dance badly.' If I sing someone will say, 'you sing badly.' If I get drunk and fight I'm sure I will lose, even if the person is smaller than me. I don't want to risk it. What it comes down to is that I only want to be in situations where I am convinced the outcome will be in my favor. I want to know the outcome; I want to have the situation firmly placed in my hand. Life must be under control. I must know that the situation will not get out of control, because when things get out of control people get hurt."

"You might get hurt?"

"Yes, I might get hurt."

"So you have no excuse. There is no philosophy determining your actions. All the books you've ever read have not led you to this state of despair and fear. It is just that you're a control freak?"

"I suppose so."

"Do you have this situation under control?"

"Yes."

"You are really and truly a fucked-up person. That someone so observant, so analytical, so calculating could end up such a dismal creature…but perhaps that is the fate of those creatures. They end up alone, consumed by their own analysis."

"Now you sound like me."

"Well, even though you've driven yourself into madness, you do still have a cute face, if that makes up for anything."

I laugh and say, "Thanks."

We talk more but it goes nowhere. It is not dramatic. It is like a person that knew me who has left and gotten a third person perspective on my life, then returned like a ghost to show me how I am at fault for what I've done.

Another thing that mildly disturbs me is that we will always be linked. Spending seven years with someone links you to them. If they do something great and die, you will be mentioned in their biography. Or to say it a different way, you go to college for four years and for the rest of your life you are a graduate of blank university. When you are with someone for a long time I suppose it is like that. You are an alumni to that person. It is like your family, how you have spent so much time with them, learned all their quirks, seen them cry, seen their happiest and shittiest moments, seen them vulnerable and heard them fart and smelled their shit. Everyone has public identities, the persona they give to the world. But everyone also has that in-the-house persona, that what-they-do-when-no-one-is-looking persona. And if you spend a lot of time with someone, that public persona wears away. And the when-no-one-is-looking persona appears, which is always vulnerable and often silly. People always remember who they have let in to that persona, to that piece of them they don't show, that is a fictionalized character fabricated to deal with the insanity of the world, so they can stay strong and determined to deal with everyday life. Which is probably the origin of the phrase people love to say concerning their lovers: 'You don't know him or her like I do.' Which is true, we don't. I don't know if it is special or unique, or whatever Hallmark shit some people throw at it. But I know that those people you get to know closely live in your mind. They don't leave you. They are always there, and you hope in some strange way that nothing bad happens to them.

VISITING
MY SISTER

On the way back to Youngstown we pass the cemetery where my sister is buried. My sister Lizaveta killed herself three years ago when she was thirty-three. She slit her wrists in a bathtub and let herself bleed to death while listening to Metallica's "Fade to Black" on repeat. We weren't really that close. I remember when I was little, around seven or eight: I was bouncing a tennis ball off the side of the garage on a normal summer day and Lizaveta ran up from behind and grabbed the tennis ball before I caught it. She held the tennis ball in one hand above my head and yelled while laughing in Russian, "Get the ball, Vasily! Get the ball, Vasily! Get the ball, Vasily!" I kept jumping and jumping, but she wouldn't give me the ball. Then she started hitting my head with the ball while laughing. Another time I was alone in the living room watching *Transformers*, my favorite cartoon, and Lizaveta came in and took the remote controller from me and switched the station. I yelled, "Put that back on!" She yelled back in Russian, "What are you going to do about it!" So I got up and tackled her but she was eighteen and I was eight so she won. Then to top it off she gave me a wedgie and laughed hysterically as I walked around the house tucking my underwear back in my pants while crying. Lizaveta and I had a lot of good times together.

"Turn into that cemetery," I say.

"Why?" Chang says.

"I want to visit my sister."

"Oh."

Chang turns into the cemetery. I tell him where to go. He drives slowly amongst the gravestones. The ground is covered in snow and it is two degrees outside. The wind is blowing hard and it feels like twenty below.

"Stop here."

Chang stops the car.

"Do you want me to come with you?" Chang says.

"No, just give me a minute."

I walk on the frozen snow. It crunches beneath my feet. I walk up to the grave. It says her name. In movies people talk to the grave. I don't talk. I can't just talk to stone. I don't believe in an afterlife. Lizaveta is dead. That is the context of the situation. I am alive and Lizaveta is dead. I can still move, my heart still beats, and Lizaveta's heart has stopped. Lizaveta is no more. Lizaveta can no longer influence the course of events on the earth. She lives in the past tense. I am, and she was. Those are the facts.

I think I am standing at her grave because it reminds me she is dead. Some days I think I will see her, like I will walk into my parents' house and she will be sitting at the kitchen table drawing little pictures in a notebook, smoking a cigarette, or I will be sitting in the Waffle House and she will just walk in and sit down next to me. Sometimes I look into other cars while I'm driving to see if she is in one of them. When the phone rings I think it might be her, or when I hear a knock on the door. But it is never her. There is no more Lizaveta. I will never see her open a Christmas present again, I will never hear her yell at me in Russian again, I will never walk into a bar and see her sitting at a table having a beer. No, death has silenced her. Her existence is absolute silence. The earth does not speak of her. The earth has swallowed her six feet below. Lizaveta is dead. And death means your existence is silenced. You can never speak again. You can never influence or affect the way of the world again. You can never enjoy again.

To be honest, I didn't really know my sister. When I was born she was ten and was moving on into puberty and had things to do. She began living her life when I started walking. She was predominately more Russian than me. When we came over, I was five and still a child and she was fifteen. She had friends in Russia; she had a life and a world back in Russia. I had nothing back in Russia. I don't even remember that place. But she did. She still spoke Russian regularly and never bothered to learn the English language well. But it doesn't matter now; she doesn't speak at all anymore. Lizaveta is dead.

Before she killed herself, times were getting rough for her. She started getting weirder and weirder. She started talking to herself in her room. She kept getting paranoid that people at work were out to get her, that they were devising huge complex plans to get her fired. She thought the government was watching her. She thought her house was bugged. She told her boyfriend of eight years to go fuck himself without any real reason. She started not leaving her house. She would go to work, do the work demanded of her, and return to her house to not speak to anyone. We all knew it was weird. We all knew that something was wrong. That perhaps she went mad. But we couldn't say it out loud. How do you say out loud, "My sister has gone mad." And to bring it farther, how do you tell your sister or any family member to their face, "Honey, you've gone crazy and we need to do something with you." You can't say things like that to people. You can't tell people to their face they've gone crazy. It is like when you see your friend date some horrible person, you can't just be like, "Joe, your girlfriend is a horrible bitch." You can't do it. Or when one of your friends gets pregnant and you know for sure they aren't ready to have a baby and that perhaps through little messages they show they don't really want one, you can't say, "Sherry, don't have that fucking baby. Get a damn abortion!" You can't do it. You just can't do it. And even if you did, they wouldn't listen.

I once saw this nature show about zebra migration patterns. The zebras had to cross this river in Africa to migrate, but crocodiles knew that zebras would be there. And all the crocodiles sat there in the water waiting for them. The zebras began to cross the river and the crocodiles started snatching them up, killing dozens of them. A lot of zebras made it across the river but a lot died. The nature show host said something like, "I hate to see these zebras get killed like this. And we could do something to help them as humans. But this is nature. This is how things are done in nature and we can't intervene." That is how I feel when I'm in that situation. My friend dating the horrible person, the person having the baby, and Lizaveta. It is nature and I cannot intervene. Either they are eaten by crocodiles or they make it across the river. Sometimes people wake up and see what they are doing and how it is leading to pain, or they don't, and they get eaten. Lizaveta was eaten. She killed herself. Her madness led her to death. We tried, well some of us tried, my mother didn't try, and my father doesn't have a clue how to be gentle. But Sasha and I tried to hint to her to get some help, to find some way of making her life better or something. But you can't tie someone down and make them do the right thing. You can't force other people into being happy or being normal or caring about themselves. There's that phrase, "No one even said life would be easy." Which is true. No one ever said that to me. No teacher ever said after teaching me how to do division, "Now class, nine divided by three is three, and life will be easy." No, no one ever said that. A philosopher didn't say that or a novelist or a poet, it was probably some guy working at some shitty job, and someone started bitching and he said in response to that guy's bitching, "No one ever said life would be easy."

As I stand here on frozen snow with twenty-below wind chill chapping my cheeks, I'm thinking, "Life is not fucking easy." Lizaveta is dead. I want her alive. I want her to stand by me and say something. I don't care what, just something like, "Hey bubblefuck." That would be enough. "Hey bubblefuck." But she isn't. She says nothing. Nothing but silence comes from her grave. She is down there rotting in a little expensive box. I am up here standing on frozen snow. The world has gone on without Lizaveta. We remain above ground working and paying bills, while she remains underground doing nothing.

A week before she killed herself, she wrote me an email. I don't know why she wrote me an email. She rarely ever communicated her feelings to me. It said:

Dear Vasily,

I'm not sure, people, they want things. Things, things, things, they want them. People, not bad, I don't know. They are always trying to get what they want, they move toward their goal, if it be great, or small, or just to be lazy. They move to it. They don't care if you are in their way, they walk over you. They bump into you, making people hate themselves. They hurt my feelings. My feelings Vasily. My feelings are everywhere, scattered, bursting, exploding, deranged, on the floor and up on the roof, my feelings. I can't find them anymore, they appear under the seat in my car, at red lights, and while eating an ice cream cone. My feelings flowing, popping up and down, and out there in the stores and at the jobs, on sidewalks, they, like scorpions, like stones, cinder blocks, and reptiles, they come and chew at my feelings. We are bursting with emotion, but we pretend we are shells. Everyone that has ever pissed me off, ever rejected me, ever dropped a grenade into the core of my heart feels like I do. I know they do. They are out there right now, feeling, the emotion, the anguish, the fear, the fear, the fear, the fear, the fear, there is so much fear, it is like a fog, a mist, an engulfing smoke that filters into our pores, into our bodies, giving us constipation of Being. My feelings Vasily, I have them, I am your older sister and I have them, you are my younger brother, you have them, we go down, in hell, in the land of snow and pig iron, humidity, and gunshots, the end is nigh, I'm being poetic, but I have to hide my emotions, while sharing them. I have to reveal and not tell, but I want to tell. I want to say like Rimbaud, "I'm suffering, I'm really suffering." Where is Rimbaud? Dead, underground, one legged. At least he had one great love; I've never loved, with passion, with wild nights and thrills. Us, postmodern children cannot love like that. All the cars are broken; the junkyards are full, guarded by men with grease under their fingertips. We are there, like rusty metal, no one is coming, no happiness can be found now. I chose to love nature, to let the sun shine on my face, to look up at tall trees, to be fascinated by the trot of the deer. To be enthralled by the beauty of the human face, not by expensive watches, expensive cars, expensive dresses, haircuts that make me look like a certain movie star. I do not know how to cook.

I'm a Russian woman, I'm equal. American women say they are equal, but they bow, they give up their arms and legs and allow chains and servitude to wreck their Being, oh, the night, and the darkness, will it not consume me, take me, my eyes, and my mouth, give me something besides the look of gloom and want of something expensive to show their friends on these faces. Their faces devoid, empty shells, faces that have memorized how to act in certain situations to appear normal, to get through days, to appear like they are people driven by the American Dream, by the Dream to own forever and ever, history has ended and it ends with the word *expensive*. I swear these humans, and they are humans, there is something human about all of them, when no one is looking, it comes, but when someone enters their presence, the gestures of a robot return. These humans would wear shit for eyeliner if it was expensive. I cannot bow before this earth, I will not debase myself before these humans who have chosen the adjective *expensive* as a God, they have deified celebrities and ruined their own emotions. They degrade themselves and call it happiness. Oh, Vasily, I am here, still on this earth, amongst humans that have chosen against happiness. I am an insoluble person, Vasily. I cannot mix. You stick me in a crowd of thousands and I make not one friend. Everyone is scared of me because I have emotion, because I am not afraid to admit that I am human, that I shit and fart, and have wet the bed. I go into public, stand and say, 'I have wet the bed!' And they run, they run from me like the boogie man. To people the boogie man is truth. Children realize in the middle of the night alone in their beds that their parents do not love them, that the world is unfair, cruel, and that the world, the only world they know is trying to grind them down into unimaginative workers who love the expensive above all else. That is the boogie man, that first fear of anguish, of knowing that you have been condemned to a life that is out of your control. They have freedom, but modern life is structured in such a way that you can only use freedom to choose what soda you drink and what to order at restaurants. But everything else has been chosen for you. Who your parents are, where you are born, how your parents treat you, what school system you go to, what economic class you are from, what neighborhood you grow up in, all chosen for you. And those are the things that make us who we are. We get our reality from the outside, and we don't get to choose the outside until we're older, and most of us are destroyed by that outside before we get a chance. Oh, chance, oh emotion, I'm not making sense, but who's trying to make sense here. People, even if they are trying to make sense, go as far as the cause, and as they approach the reason, the core of the problem, they realize they are part of the reason, and give up, they stop at the cause, because the cause is simple. The reasons terrify them. I decided one day to go to the reasons, to smash all nonsense and grab the reason and pull it down and hold it in my hand, and let it terrify me. And I have been alone ever since. I have been alone for so long, so long without anyone that can understand what I'm trying to explain, trying to get out of this Russian body of mine. But I have received only silence. A silence that screams at me, 'Just die please, you are ruining my day.' I cannot take it anymore. I cannot take this anymore, I cannot, I cannot, I cannot, I cannot, this world, these people with their expensive faces have demolished me, have made me falter and now my legs have given out, my Being sways like the willows, and the swamp has engulfed me, there is nothing left to give, I have given and not received, I wanted happiness. I swear, there was a piece of me that woke up every morning and said, 'I want to be happy today.' Then they would send their dogs out and they will attack me, bite, scratch, tear at my Being until there was nothing left but to resign myself to this misery. I'm not alone in this suffering, in this bleakness, but what hurts most is that they won't admit it in unity, they won't just say to each other that they feel it too, and that is what hurts most, is that I'm alone, but I'm not.

See ya sometime,

Lizaveta.

Chang walks up behind me. I hear his feet crunching the snow. He stands beside me, puts his hand on my shoulder and says, "She's dead."

I stand there for a minute and say, "Yeah, it's cold. Let's get out of here."

We walk back to the car, in silence.

TWO HARD
WORKERS

One's name was Josiah. Josiah was not very smart. The most common thing said about him was, "I think he might have brain damage." Josiah was a hard worker but not a good worker. At the concentration camp they were forced to make boots for the Nazis and Josiah kept messing up and causing problems for the other workers. People were always saying, "We're in a concentration camp probably to die at any moment, and Josiah is making things worse for us."

The other's name was Yosef. Yosef was a hard and good worker. But Yosef never stopped talking. Yosef would start talking as soon as he woke up till the second he went to sleep. Yosef didn't need anyone to respond to anything he said. He would keep talking no matter what. People were always telling Yosef to shut up but Yosef never listened. People often said of Yosef, "Why won't he shut up, we are so miserable, life is so hard, and he keeps talking."

Yosef would also do things like if he stepped on a nail and got cut he would go around telling everyone how he got his foot cut and people would reply, "Yosef, we're in a fucking concentration camp waiting to die, who cares about a little cut." Yosef wouldn't respond to that though, and would go on telling everyone about his cut foot.

Yosef also made friends with the Nazis. He would talk to the Nazi bosses and try to make friends with them. People would tell him, "Yosef, the Nazis hate us. They're laughing at you."

Yosef would respond, "No, the Nazis love me."

People would walk away in anger.

Josiah though made great potato soup with very little ingredients. Josiah would prepare the soup and everyone would feast and people would say, "Josiah messes up a lot, but he does make great soup."

One day there was no food. And many were close to starvation, so Josiah took it upon himself, maybe because of empathy, bravery, or because he actually had brain damage, to steal some food.

Josiah crawled through deep snow and through barb wire in the night to break into the Nazi food supplies. Josiah broke into the supply shed and got out one box and pushed it slowly through mud and snow while crawling for over two hours back to the barracks for people to eat, knowing the whole time if he were caught it would be the last thing he ever did.

Everyone was so hungry they chewed on the uncooked potatoes in the night. Yosef, though, did not eat the potatoes. He went to the Nazi bosses and told them what Josiah did.

The Nazis marched in the barracks where the starving Jews were. The Nazis grabbed the potatoes from their starving fingers. One Nazi ripped the food out of a small girl's mouth. The Nazis shot Josiah in the head. Josiah lay there still and quiet never to mess up at work again. The starving Jews looked at dead Josiah, the person that tried to save them who they always said had brain damage. Then they looked up at Yosef standing next to the Nazis. Yosef stood smiling with not an ounce of remorse on his face.

The Nazis shot all the starving Jews that ate the potatoes. They lay there dying. Their waiting was over. In their last moments they didn't know who to blame: Josiah for stealing, Yosef for snitching, or the Nazis. They bled to death before they could decide on someone to blame.

The Nazis never killed Yosef. Yosef lived through the war and still lives. No one ever knew Yosef did that. The starving Jews were dead and the Russians killed the Nazis there that night.

After the war was over, Yosef went to America and became a successful businessman. He got married and divorced several times and had several kids. He can be found in Florida living in a retirement community getting a tan next to a pool.

www.ingramcontent.com/pod-product-compliance
Lightning Source LLC
Chambersburg PA
CBHW031235260626
47169CB00007B/2305